Two Fisted Tales of Times Square

Pete Chiarella

Published by 42nd Street Pete, 2022.

This is a work of fiction. Similarities to real people, places, or events are entirely coincidental.

TWO FISTED TALES OF TIMES SQUARE

First edition. October 25, 2022.

Copyright © 2022 Pete Chiarella.

ISBN: 979-8223753179

Written by Pete Chiarella.

Table of Contents

INTRODUCTION 1
TWO FISTED TALES OF TIMES SQUARE 2
CLOSED FOREVER 24
THE AMATEURS 31
A CONFLICT OF INTEREST 44
BUSTED 61
TERRIBLE TOM 71
WRONG PLACE, WRONG TIME 79
THE FIXER 93
THE ACQUISITION 111
THE MUTT 124
RETRIBUTION 129
TEDDY'S PLACE 137
THE BLIZZARD 152
SLAMBURGER 167

INTRODUCTION

When I first started the journey of journalism, I was writing about movies for publications like Shock Cinema, Uncut, Screw, Chiller Theatre, Ultraviolent and others. Then I started Grindhouse Purgatory and wrote A Whole Bag of Crazy. This isn't my first shot at fiction. A few years ago, I wrote Gunfighters of the Drunken Master which became a trilogy.

Jack Ketchum was a friend and mentor to me. He wrote me saying that he always wondered when I would try my hand at fiction. He loved the Gunfighters stuff and advised me on certain things to make me a better writer. I was thinking about a bunch of stories loosely based on things that I saw or was involved in back on 42nd Street in the 70's.

This is the end result.

I used locations like Blackjack Books, Club 44, McGirr's Pool Hall, Club 45, The Terminal Bar, The Liberty Theater and other places. The characters are based on people that I knew, dealt with or knew enough about them to stay away. The language that I use is the language that we spoke back then. I know that it may be offensive to the overly sensitive. Too bad, I don't change history, I just write about it.

It was a rough, dangerous time, filled with rough, dangerous people. But, unlike today, you were alive, you did what you wanted to, as long as you could get away with it. I make no apologies for the language or the content. It was a wonderful time that a lot of people fondly remember. You get a little bit of everything here, horror, action, crime, murder and mobsters. I hope you enjoy the ride.

Dedicated to my friend, the late, great Jack Ketchum, missing you terribly Dallas, glad we had that one last drink together.

• • • •

PETE CHIARELLA
February 14, 2022

TWO FISTED TALES OF TIMES SQUARE

The following story is a concoction of actual events, rumors, and things personally witnessed during my time on 'The Deuce'. The early 80's was twisted, violent times and the end of an era was soon to occur. The 'rot' in the big apple was in full effect here. The 80's brought the area the AIDS crisis, a new drug called crack, and vulture like realtors who saw dollar signs as the area fell into decay. Within the next decade, it would be all over. The pulse of 42nd Street was faint, theaters closed up one by one. Beat drug salesmen operated out of shuttered alcoves. Zombie like crack addicts shuffled about looking for someone to rob. A psychopath was stalking and murdering hookers during this time period. The entire area was in its death throes.

So, this is a semi fictional tale of strange events that occurred. I had the idea for a werewolf/bounty hunter years ago. The original manuscript was lost, but it stuck in my head until I decided to play around with it. The following tale is how I incorporated a fictional character into some real events.

• • • •

SOMEWHERE IN EASTERN EUROPE IN THE 1700's
THE 12-YEAR-OLD BOY ran through the forest ahead of his pursuers. They were out for blood, his blood. The boy, Nickolas Strankovitch, had been attacked a month prior to this, by what appeared to be a wolf. His left shoulder had been savaged and a five-pointed star remained. The elders of his village felt he was cursed. They felt he was evil and that the next full moon would bring death to their village.

The leaders had a meeting. During that meeting they all agreed that the boy should be put to death. The boy's mother, however, wasn't going to let that happen. She packed up what little provisions she had and told the boy he had to leave.

"You're not safe here", she told him. "Go," she said, "Get far from this place, and you'll be safe." The boy left.

When confronted by the angry leaders of the village, she was silent.

"You will give us the boy, or you will die in his place," they told her.

"I will never give you my son," she told them. She was beaten down, then dragged to the village square. She was tied to a stake.

"I'll give you one chance to tell us where he is, or you will burn," one of the elders told her. She spit in his face. Her people burned her alive that night.

The boy felt a strange sense of loss, but his pursuers were catching up to him. A full moon was rising, a sharp pain shot through the boy's head. The pain's intensity dropped the boy to his knees. He felt horrible pain as his bones broke and rearranged, contorting his body. His jaws elongated and his teeth fell out only to be replaced with sharp incisors and fangs. A terrible rage enveloped his mind, he saw red, then he saw no more.

Morning dawned, the boy awoke shivering in the cold. His clothes were in tatters around him. He was covered in blood and none of it his. He was confused. There was a trail of blood. He followed it. He found the shredded remains of four men, his pursuers. All dead, ripped to pieces. Nicholas knew that this was his work, and he knew he was cursed, or was he? Nicholas was an intelligent boy and was not going to accept what fate put upon him.

Nicholas became the demon of the forest, wrecking violent death to anyone with the intention of ferreting him out. He also learned something. He learned that he could control the change. It took a while and a lot of trial and error, but the boy eventually mastered it. But the bloodlust still called to him. Over time, he would rid his psyche of that desire, but now it was time to leave Europe. He could also never love. At times, he did love, he took a gypsy girl as a bride. But watching her grow old and withered, while he never changed, caused him heart break. He would take a lover, pay a prostitute, but never really fall in love again.

Nicholas wound up on a ship headed to the new world, America. He arrived in time for The Revolution. He was quick to join. Then came the Civil War, then two World wars, then Korea, then Vietnam. On the battlefield, what was a few more mutilated bodies? The wars covered up Nicholas's penchant for bloodlust. Nicholas was highly decorated for his 'sanctions" behind enemy lines. He was the best and retired from the service.

He started a 'service' of sorts. One, he was a skip tracer who would pick up guys that jumped bail. Two, he was an assassin for hire. Only he wouldn't stoop to low level murder for profit. If he took a contract, the person had to be completely evil, supposedly above the law. He became the avenging angel for those who could afford him. He also mastered the change. He didn't turn into a monster unless he had to. His superhuman strength was all he needed.

• • • •

NEW YORK CITY EARLY 1980's

Willie Morton was the son of Walter Morton, millionaire businessman. He was 23, short, chubby, and bespeckled. He had been entrusted a piece of business by his father. It was his time to close the deal and be part of the Morton Empire. He had met his contact in a posh, Midtown Hotel. The meeting went well, and a deal was cut. Willie was elated. He was having a drink in the hotel bar when he saw her.

She had dark, Mediterranean features. Her eyes projected a smoldering sensuality. Her body was tight, well-muscled, yet totally feminine. And she was looking at him. He shyly asked her to join him for a drink. She accepted. They made small talk for a bit. Willie excused himself to use the facilities.

When he returned, there was a fresh drink waiting for him. More small talk led to an invitation to go to her room. They got up to leave, Willie felt odd. They were almost to the bank of elevators when Willie's vision started to blur. He felt like he was falling. Strong arms held him up, then darkness fell.

Willie woke up, he was not in his hotel room. He was in a dark room and was very cold. He felt something on his chest. It was a note that said, "Call 911". Willie was naked and, in a bathtub, full of ice. He looked down and saw that he was packed in ice. There were incisions on his lower abdomen. He started screaming and, in his mind, the screaming never stopped.

• • • •

1

I ARRIVED IN NEW YORK City late in the evening. I had been contacted about a job that would have a big payoff. My rather opulent hotel room was paid for. I was told to check in and I would be contacted. There was a message waiting for me. I was given an address on Park Avenue and was asked to call when I got settled. Not wanting to waste time, I called Mr. Morton. I was told a car would be coming to pick me up shortly. The bell captain called and told me a car was waiting for me. I got into a brand-new Continental and was driven to a Park Avenue mansion.

Walter Morton was around fifty but looked years older. He ushered me into his study and offered me refreshment. After sampling some exquisite bourbon, we talked business.

"You come highly recommended, Mr. Strankovitch," Morton began.

"Just call me Nick," I said.

"I understand you have a situation that needs to be resolved. I need your complete discretion on this matter," Morton told me.

"Mr. Morton, any job I take I ensure complete discretion. Whatever conversation takes place here, rest assured, it will never leave this room."

That placated Morton. "I had sent my son, William, to close a business transaction," he explained. "After that transaction was taken care of, Willie decided to have a celebratory drink in the hotel bar. According to the bar tender, he struck up a conversation with some woman." Morton continued. "The bartender recalled that Willie appeared to be either drunk or sick. The woman and some fellow helped him out of the bar. Shortly after that, my son was found in a bathtub in The Green Lantern Motel on 8th Avenue. His kidneys and liver had been cut out of him."

My eyebrows raised at this bit of information. I let him continue.

"Willie lost his mind, the shock of what happened destroyed him. I lost my son last week, Nick," Morton finished. "I want revenge, Nick, revenge that I will pay very well for."

"Tell me what you need done," I asked him, although I had a pretty good idea of what he wanted.

"I hired some people who did some leg work already. Willie wasn't the only one this happened to. Several prostitutes and some transients have been found in the same condition. There is a ring operating in my city that is stealing and selling human organs."

"And my role in your revenge," I asked.

"I will give you every bit of information I have gathered" Morton told me "I want them all dead, every last one involved in this, and especially the bitch who set my son up."

Morton took out a check book and wrote out a check. He slid it over to me. "Is that enough to retain your services and assure your discretion in this matter," he asked. I looked at the amount, it was for five hundred thousand dollars.

"There will be another check for the same amount after you finish the job. Do we have a deal, sir?"

"We do," I told him. "I'll need every bit of information you have, including the names and whereabouts of any potential witnesses."

"That you shall have, when can you start?"

"I'll start tonight," I told him. "The trail might be cold now, but not that cold that I can't pick it up."

• • • •

2

I FIGURED THE BEST place to start would be the bar where Willie met the woman. The hotel was on 8th Avenue between West 29th and 28th Street. The upscale lounge was located a few steps down, beneath the hotel. I ordered my usual Makers and water. I asked the bartender if he was always on this shift. He gave me a suspicious glance.

"Yeah," he replied, "this is my shift."

"There was a guy in here two weeks ago, bookish guy, remember him?"

"Mister," he started. "I see different people in here every night. That's not a lot for me to go on."

"How about the fact that he left with a piece of ass that usually wouldn't give him the time of day?"

The bartender thought a bit. "You a cop," he asked.

"No, just a guy paid to find something out," I told him. "Maybe this will jog your memory." I slid a ten spot across the bar. He took the bill.

"Alright," he said. "The guy was here, and this chic hit on him. She was probably a high rolling pro. The guy got a little tanked and she put him in a cab."

"Did she go with him," I asked.

He thought a bit. "Yeah, she must have, because she didn't come back in."

"Has she been in here before," I asked.

"She's not what I would call a regular, but she has been in here a couple of times."

I handed him my card with my pager number on it. "If she comes in, page me, that ten spot becomes a C-note if you can do that," I told him.

"Ok, you have a deal," he replied, "But I don't want any shit splattering on me," he said.

"No worries, we never had this conversation."

I finished my drink and went looking for some answers. Answers could be had for a price. Most denizens of the tenderloin were not prone to polite conversation unless something was in it for them. But I knew one guy who would talk, so now I was headed to one of the worst places on 42nd Street, Blackjack Books.

Blackjack Books was a mob run boil on the butt of 42nd street. Located midway up the block, it was open 24/7. The night manager was a guy known as Tondawanda Pete. A surly bastard who, after one or two tours of Vietnam, turned sour on the human race. Pete pretty much knew all the dark secrets of who was doing what and to who. No one knew where he lived. He kept a cot in the back room to crash out on when things got slow. He had two thugs working there as 'security' and a few girls of questionable health, working the live peep booths.

I took the subway to 42nd and 8th. I hated walking that tunnel between the station to get to 42nd Street. It was a mugger's paradise this time of night. Scumbags would break the overhead lights and wait in the shadows. Just my luck that there were three assholes looking to take someone off. Not too subtle, they surround me. One thing I don't need right now is a pile of bodies. One comes at me with a knife out.

"Just give us your wallet, homie, then you can walk." He gives me a smile full of gold teeth. Those teeth fly out of his mouth like gold Chicklets as I back handed him. The other two rush me. I break one's arm and send him headfirst into the wall. The last guy claws a Saturday

Night Special from his pocket. I grab the gun hand and squeeze it, breaking his fingers.

Now the three are on the ground in various states of pain. "Enjoy the rest of your evening," I tell them.

I emerge from the subway on the left-hand side of the block. The 24/7 porn grinder, The Harem has 'Four Continuous Features'. The martial arts store is doing a thriving business as the Kung Fu craze hasn't faded away yet. I pass The Liberty Theater which has the double bill of Make Them Die Slowly and Demonoid. Three black guys are running a three-card monte scam close to Blackjacks. As I go into the store, I hear Pete bellowing orders to Leon, his security guard. "Go tell these niggers to move that fuckin game somewhere else"

"Ok boss," Leon replies. Leon learned not to question Pete. One of the hustlers follows Leon back in.

"Hey motherfucker, you don't own the street, so fuck off, we aren't moving."

Pete motions the guy closer. "Say what?"

"You heard me, you bitch ass punk, we aint..." Pete grabs him by the front of his shirt and sticks a 357 magnum under his chin.

"You want to give me a problem, you worthless piece of shit? I'll waste your black ass and toss you in the river. Now get the fuck out of my face". Pete shoves the guy away. The guy, actually shaking, sulks out.

I clap my hands, "Bravo," I tell him.

Pete looks at me. "Oh, fuck, look who's back in town, long time, Nick."

"Still have that sunny disposition, right Pete?"

"Comes with the territory working here," Pete replied. "What brings you back to Fun City?"

"A little job," I tell him. "Looking for some information."

Pete's eyes narrow. "What kind of information," he asks.

"Seems some hot little piece of ass is setting guys up," I tell him.

Pete snorts a laugh. "That ain't nothin' new, bitches always set guys up for a little robbery."

"Yeah," I reply, "I know that, but how many steal a guy's kidneys?"

"Are you fuckin serious," Pete asks.

"Yeah, serious enough for getting a nice payday from a victim's father," I tell him.

"So, you're on the hunt, Nick?"

"I have a lead, the bar the kid got picked up in."

I slipped Pete a $20 bill. "Let me know if anything shakes loose and buy yourself dinner."

"Will do," Pete replied.

· · · ·

3

IT DIDN'T TAKE VERY long for things to shake out. The following morning, Nick had a visitor. It was Pete's man, Leon.

"Pete has something for you, can you meet him at the store?"

"Sure, what time?"

"Around noon would be good."

"Any idea what he has?"

"Not sure, but something happened that has certain people shook up."

"Tell him I'll be there."

Leon nodded then left.

Nick arrived at Blackjack Books at noon. Pete was waiting. So was another guy, and this guy wasn't your standard peepshow aficionado. "Nick, this is Joey."

Joey was well dressed in a black suit. He had 'mob' written all over him. The two shook hands.

"We have interests that coincide," Joey explained.

"How so," Nick asked.

"The best way to explain it is to show you something. You have heard about snuff films, right?"

"That urban legend, yeah, I have heard rumblings."

"Well the catholic church created that rumor to mess with our business. So, we made fake films to capitalize on it. I'll show you."

Pete cued an 8mm projector. A couple hook up and go to an obvious motel room. They have sex for the length of that reel, then reel two kicks in. More of the same until the last minute or so where a big guy kicks in the door and stabs the girl with a fake knife. A lot of fake blood, then it ends.

"Well that was special," Nick remarked.

"I know it's a sucker's trap. It would cost nine dollars in quarters to see it to the end. It's fake, but this one isn't."

Pete starts another reel. This one has a girl tied up and suspended. She is getting whipped by another girl. Blood drips down her back. The camera pans on her terrified face. She has a ball gag in her mouth. The girl now has a steak knife and puts it in the girl's vagina and starts sawing upwards.

"Turn it the fuck off," Joey tells Pete.

Pete has a look of total disgust on his face.

Joey addresses Nick. "This is not what we do, we make and sell fuck films, we don't murder people."

"So where do our interests coincide," Nick asked.

"You're looking for a person or persons that stole that kids' organs."

This is part of it. We know that someone connected to our business made this film. We can't allow this. We know who it is, and we are going to take care of it."

"So where do I come in?"

"You find out who is buying the organs and put them out of business. I was sent to help you do it, but you are going to need more help."

"You can supply that help?"

"No, I'm it, they are taking care of our in-house problem, you need to take care of the rest of it. And don't tell me you can't afford it, we know better."

Pete interrupted further conversation. "There's going to be another problem, that girl we just saw in the film, I know who she is."

"Who is she," Joey asked.

"Her name is Lisa; she works the live sex show at The Doll."

"So, she was one of ours?"

"Yeah, and her best friend is Will Ferris."

"Who is Will Ferris," Nick asked.

"A fellow Nam vet who has terminal cancer," Pete replied. "He got exposed to Agent Orange and it's killing him. Lisa was his only friend."

"Will he be a problem?"

"He won't be an asset, that's for sure."

"Why is that?"

"He uses PCP to kill the pain, he's unstable and dangerous."

"Best we steer clear of him, you have anyone in mind as to extra help?"

Joey thought for a moment.

"I know two guys, Nails Morgan and Cueball Jones. They would be interested."

"Nails, how did he get that name, because he's tough as a nail?"

"No, although he is that tough. What happened was he was drunk and broke. Someone made him a bet that he couldn't drive a nail into the bar with his fist. The crazy bastard took six of those flat head nails, then pounded them into the bar with his head. His forehead is a mess."

"Ok, what about this Cueball guy?"

"Jones is a black guy, he does some collections for some bookies, things like that. If there's a problem, he takes Nails with him. I think they met in the joint. Nails isn't too smart, so Jones watches out for him."

"So where do we find these gentlemen?"

"McGirr's Pool Hall, Club 44, or the Metropole when they have money."

"So, let's go have a word with these guys."

• • • •

4

WE STRUCK OUT AT MCGIRR'S.

"They were here, but they left a couple of hours ago," Pop the cook told them. "Try Club 44, I don't think they got thrown out of there lately."

So, we go to Club 44. A sign by the door tells patrons about their bouncer, Nino Valdez, a former boxer. I checked out Nino, he is one big guy. But there was a loud argument going on at the end of the bar. A skinny guy, with a huge afro, was yelling at a guy with a scarred face, Nails Morgan. "You honky faggot, you show The Hawk some respect," the guy yelled.

"I know three guys that call themselves The Hawk," Nails snarled. "One of them is a skip tracer for Lou's Bail Bonds out of Jersey City. Another has a policy bank over in Harlem. The last one is a boss in the Bloods Gang, so no, you ain't the Hawk. You might be The Sparrow, or The Robin, but you ain't the fuckin Hawk."

The Hawk tried to pull something out of his pocket. An uppercut hit his chin and 'The Hawk' hit the floor, out cold. Cueball picked up the knife he almost pulled.

"Wow, it's a 007 knife." Jones held it up, the blade wobbled.

Nino walked up to Jones, took the knife, stuck it into the bar, then broke the blade off.

Nails said to Nino, "Yeah, I know, we're eighty-sixed again." Nino just grunted and pointed to the door.

"See you next week," Jones told Nino as the two walked out the door.

Joey intercepted them. "I need a word, guys".

"So, talk," Nails said.

"Not here, let's go to club 45, they have a backroom we can use."

Club 45 was on the next block. Its claim to fame was that scenes from Midnight Cowboy and The Owl and the Pussycat were shot there. A big sign told potential customers that. Other than that notoriety, it was just another shot and beer joint. Joey motioned to the bartender that they would be using the backroom. A round of drinks were ordered as they settled in. Joey opened the conversation.

"We have a job that needs to be done, it's a good payday, but it's going to be dangerous."

"How dangerous," Cueball interjected.

"Fatally if it goes south."

Nails and Cueball looked at each other.

"Give us the particulars," Jones asked.

"Ok Nick, you're up."

I stood up. "Here's the story. I was hired to find out who drugged someone's only son and stole his kidneys. Some hot looking bitch drugged him in a hotel bar. I already talked to the bartender as to give me a heads up if she shows up. Then Joey shows me a film where one of the local dancers is being killed. The set-up girl killed her. Someone is shooting snuff films and selling organs on the black market. Joey's boss is taking care of one part of the problem, Joey and I have to resolve the other part of the problem. I'm being paid to the effect that no one involved is going to walk away. So, there will be violence and I'll pay you each 10K to help."

"Ten thousand bucks," gasped Nails, "I could pay off all my tabs, maybe have some..."

"No," Jones interrupted. "Only you could piss that kind of cash away in a week. I'll manage it for you."

"Cool, we can go to the track, or maybe Vegas..."

"Not that kind of managing, Nails, you know you suck when it comes to money."

Jones says, "Ok, we're in, what's the plan?"

Before I could answer a big man with crazy, bloodshot eyes, long stringy hair, and a big, dirty dog came through the door, Will Ferris.

Ferris was tall, gaunt, dirty and had crazy written all over him. The dog, a mix of Pitbull and God knows what else followed him. The dog was big, close to a hundred pounds. It had scars on its head and a blue and brown eye. It just stood there waiting. Ferris didn't wait to be asked.

"Whatever you're doing, we are in," he snarled.

"The hell you are," Joey said. "Who the hell told you?"

"I did," a voice said. Tonawanda Pete stepped into the room.

"Why the fuck did you do that?"

"His girl got killed, he has a right to even things up."

"He can hardly stand up."

"Don't talk like I'm not here," Ferris bellowed. "I'll do whatever it takes, I'm not here to get paid, I'm here to kill and die."

I looked long and hard at Ferris. The man was dead already, and his body didn't know it. I understood.

"Ok, Will, but I call the shots, what's with the dog?"

"He hung around Lisa, he's been on me like white on rice, he knows something is wrong."

"Keep him with you then, guess you can go back to work, Pete."

"Joe gave me the night off, he also lent me a car."

"That was nice of him."

"It's not for me, it's for you. You think a cab driver will hang around when shit starts?"

"No, they won't, but I will."

"Aren't you still on probation?"

"As far as anyone will know, I'm at the counter tonight."

"Fair enough."

There was a knock on the door and a well-dressed man entered the room, Detective Morelli.

"Is this a private party," he asked.

"Obviously not private enough," I said.

Morelli chuckled, "So what do we have here? 42nd Street's own Heckle and Jekyll, a Capo De Tutti Frutti, a psycho and his dog, the illustrious night manager of Blackjack Books, and you, Nick. Last time you visited our fair city, two unfortunate gentlemen were found mutilated by the East River. Then the other night, three Hispanic gentlemen claim a guy assaulted them in the subway."

I glared at him, "And your point is?"

"Look, some of us know something rotten has been going down," Morelli began. "I was sent here to tell you this, you get a pass tonight, do what you have to do, then vanish."

"Someone must be really worried about something," I said.

"Cut the bullshit, you know we can let this get out, the city has a bad enough rep. We need tourists, and we don't need these tourists vanishing. Muggings, purse snatching, drug deals, hooking, yeah, that we can deal with. People getting their organs cut out of them, no way. Get your work done, then go on vacation, all of you."

Morelli left them staring at me. Joey spoke up. "You beat three guys so bad that they are in the ER, and what's this about mutilated bodies?"

"You really want to know?"

"If I'm working with you, I have to trust you, but you're a fuckin ghost. People know you, but they don't know you. So, what are you?"

"Simple answer, I'm a werewolf."

First there was a shocked look on some faces, but then a few chuckles.

"Prove it," Pete asked, "Or do we need a full moon?"

I stood up and took off my jacket. I raised my arm and my hand started to pulse. My fingers grew longer, and nails pushed out. My hand had turned into a claw. The group was silent.

"It isn't like you see in movies and I don't have the time to explain it. I'm very old and I control it. When it first happened, not so much, but now I learned to manage it and make it work for me."

"I've seen The Wolfman over 20 times," Nails said.

"And why are you telling me that?"

"Just adding to the conversation." Jones just shook his head.

"Something else," I added, "I can't be hurt or killed in the usual ways, so don't get in front of me. Now are we all packing?" Joey had a 357 Magnum, Jones, a nine-millimeter, Pete a 45 automatic.

"What about you two," I asked Nails and Ferris. Ferris pulled out a utility knife.

"I'm takin out that bitch, I won't last much longer after that, nor do I intend to."

"Nails can't shoot," Jones announced. "Seriously," I asked.

"He sucks, he can't get the hang of it. We went to a range and were asked to leave. He hit everything but the target. Sucks because of this guilt by association crap, I can't ever go back."

"Jones, that ain't fair, some people just can't figure out certain stuff. I know how to do stuff that you don't know how to do."

"Like what?"

"Well, you know."

"No, I don't, care to enlighten the group?"

"I'm pondering on it."

"Cool, let us know when you come up with something. Bro, this isn't a situation where your fists and charm will get the job done."

"Always worked before."

"We don't have time for this shit. There's a shotgun behind the bar," Joey said. "Nails just point it at the bad guys and pull the trigger."

"And make sure the rest of us are behind you when you pull it," Jones added.

Nails glared at him, then my pager went off.

"I need a phone." I went to the pay phone in the bar. It was the bartender from the hotel. "The girl just strolled in." I told him he would be taken care of.

"The girl is at the hotel bar, three blocks from here." Joey, come with me and watch how it plays out. When she takes me, all of you follow me?" The two practically jogged to the hotel.

• • • •

5

PETE WENT AND GOT THE car, a Lincoln Town Car. Nails and Pete are in the front seats. Ferris and the dog got into the back seats. Cueball and the dog had a stare down.

"I don't think he likes me, Nails, switch seats with me."

"I'm not sure he likes anyone," Ferris said.

"He doesn't bother me, I like dogs." Nails got in the back and he and the dog stared at each other.

"You gonna bite me," Nails asked. The dog gave him a quizzical look, then licked his face. "We good".

Pete parked the car close to the hotel. "We watch and pick up Joey, then we tail them."

Me and Joey went into the bar and split up. The bartender gave me a nod. I slipped him a C-note. The girl was a stunner, long, black hair, tight body, sensuous lips, and brown eyes. I chatted her up. Her name was Marlene.

"Can I buy you a drink," I asked.

"Certainly," she replied. She was drinking a martini. "New in town?"

"Yes, first time in the Big Apple, very exciting."

"Are you here on business?"

"Yes, I'm a garment importer."

"So, you're in town alone."

"Yes, for a day or so, then on to my next appointment."

"Honey, can you get me another drink?"

"Sure thing." I flagged the bartender and Marlene spiked his drink. I thought, too bad it will have zero effect on me.

I kept up the conversation and noticed that Marlene was getting a bit nervous. I was jerking her chain, so now I started slurring a bit. I'll play the game, I started to nod out.

"Poor baby," she cooed, "guess you had a little too much."

Marlene signaled a large man who was at the end of the bar.

"Call us a cab," she instructed the bartender. Joey was up and heading for the door. He jumped into the town car.

"It's on," he told the group. "A cab's is coming, so we follow."

Marlene and the big guy muscled me into the cab. They followed the cab into Chinatown. It turned onto East Broadway, then down a side street. It stopped at a two-story building. The two got out of the cab and entered the building dragging me along.

"How do you want to play this," Pete asked.

Ferris lit a pipe, and a horrible odor filled the car. "I'll be the first wave, fuckers." He turned to Pete "Semper Fi brother." He slapped Pete five and pulled out his utility knife. "Let's go," he muttered. Ferris and the dog went into the building.

The big guy was standing in the alcove. He went to grab Ferris. Ferris cut his throat. Someone fired a shot from the top of the stairs hitting Ferris in the side. The dog charged up the stairs and knocked the gunman down, ripping out his throat. Ferris staggered up the stairs. Nails, Jones and Joey made their move.

"Pete, shoot anyone who comes out that isn't us," Joey ordered. "Nails, you stay downstairs, shoot anyone who tries to get out." Joey and Jones traded bullets with shooters as they tried to climb the stairs.

I was in a makeshift operating room when the shooting started. I jumped off the gurney, scaring the two doctors who were ready to open me up. One was Asian, the other Middle Eastern. The girl tried to stab me with a scalpel as Ferris crashed through the door. The Asian doctor pulled a gun and shot Ferris. Ferris kept on coming. He grabbed Marlene by the throat and held her off the floor. "You'll not go out easy, you fuckin cunt, this is for Lisa." Ferris shoved the utility knife in her belly and ripped her guts out. I grabbed the gun from the doctor and shot him in the head with it. The other doctor pulled out a .38.

Ferris went after him but caught five bullets in the chest. Dying, he picked the guy up and threw him out a window. Ferris looked at me. "I did it and I'm done." Ferris hit the floor with a smile on his face. Joey and Jones had a running battle going on. Jones took a slug in his right leg. Nails had cleared his area out with the shotgun, but he was out of shells. I killed everyone that came at me. There was an eerie silence as gun smoke swirled about. Joey and Jones found me.

"Let's get the fuck outta here," Jones yelled. The three men tried for the stairs, supporting Jones between them. In the lobby, a gunman was stalking Nails with a shotgun.

"Looks like you're outta of bullets, scumbag, say goodbye." Nails stared him down knowing he was dead. Then the big dog took the guy down and started chewing on his face. Nails picked up the discarded shotgun just as the elevator opened. Five armed men milled about.

Seeing what was happening, I yelled, "Shoot those bastards, Nails, pull the fucking trigger." Nails pointed the gun at the elevator and pulled the trigger.

A tongue of white fire engulfed the gunmen and set the lobby on fire. Nails dropped the gun and ran to help the others. The old building was a firetrap and was burning fast. The four got out and piled in the car. "Get us out of here, Pete." Pete floored the Lincoln.

"Ferris," Pete asked.

"He went out the way he wanted to, he got even for Lisa," I told him.

"That fire will cover our tracks," Joey said.

"Where's the mutt," Nails asked. "He saved my life, I'm going to buy him a steak, maybe a London broil."

"He took off after you lit the place up, he'll be back," Pete told him. Head into Brooklyn," Joey told Pete. "Jones needs a doctor to take that slug out of his leg."

"What the fuck was in that gun," Nails asked.

"Something called Dragon's Breath, shells loaded with white phosphorus," I replied. "Joey, pull over, I need to use a phone."

I called Morelli's number at the station. "Detective Morelli speaking."

"There's a building on fire off of East Broadway, don't hurry to put it out." I hung up.

Jones was taken to a friendly doctor who took the bullet out of his leg. I told everyone to scatter but meet me in two days at Club 45. I called Mr. Morton.

"The job is done, sir, as asked all involved have been taken care of."

"Does this have anything to do with a fire in China Town?"

"I wouldn't know, sir, I was out with friends."

"Your check will be ready when you get here."

Nails and Jones were at Club 45 waiting for me. Joey was also hanging out. I showed up with three packages and the newspaper. The headline read, 'Drug Lab in Chinatown Goes up in Flames.' The story was that the building caught fire and that fire was hard to put out. Lab equipment and guns were found in the wreckage leading authorities to believe rival dealers attacked the lab and the fire was the result of it.

"Well," said Joey. "I do believe we are in the clear."

"Yes," I said as I passed around thick envelopes. "We are. Here's the cash as promised."

"I wasn't involved in this deal," Joey said.

"I know you're getting something on the other end, consider this a bonus."

"Many thanks. I guess you're on the way out now?"

"Yeah, just one stop to make and I'm gone. Good working with you gentlemen. Maybe we can do it again sometime." Hands were shaken all around.

I went to Blackjack Books. Pete was back behind the counter. Scowling at customers. I slipped him an envelope full of cash.

"What's this," he asked.

"Something maybe to help some of your fellow vets, and maybe you. Seeing what happened to Ferris bothered me. I was a soldier once and the way the veterans are treated is bullshit. Use this to help someone, okay?"

"You're a standup guy, Nick, I appreciate this." The two shook hands and Nick left.

• • • •

The real story. Rumors started in the 80's about people being set up and drugged and had their kidneys stolen. It is an 'urban legend', but who really knows.

Snuff films were invented by The Catholic Church in their war on porn. Supposedly a woman is killed on film during sex. David Friedman told me they made 'fake' snuff films to capitalize on these rumors. The way Joey described the film is the way they were, a way to separate a sucker from his money.

Nino Valdez was the doorman/bouncer at Club 44. He was a big, quiet man who took no shit. A guy actually called the Hawk was a skip tracer that worked for a guy named Lou who had an office in Jersey City. Robert DeNiro based his character in Midnight Run on Lou who he had several meetings with.

The 007 knife was a popular piece of shit knife in the late 70's. Many Vietnam Veterans returned home damaged. Or were treated like shit because they fought in an unpopular war. Many wound up working in vice filled Times Square as bouncers for strip clubs and massage parlors, live sex show performers, or as hired muscle.

They deserved better.

CLOSED FOREVER

For decades it stood in the middle of 42nd Street in NYC, New York. Opulent in the 30's and 40's, it fell into disrepair starting in the late 60's. It would be considered a 'Grindhouse'. A theater that was open until almost dawn and 'ground out' films nonstop. Their choice of 'programming' left a lot to be desired by the people who lived and worked near it. It was The Liberty Theater.

• • • •

THE LIBERTY'S LIFE blood, the films, were some of the most violent and vile ever produced. Starting with Night of the Living Dead in 1968 and ending with the horrific Butchers of the Damned in 1986, the theater was a showcase for violence, sadism, torture, and death. Fight for Your Life, Trap Them and Kill Them, Make Them Die Slowly, Cut-Throats Nine and Cannibal Holocaust all played there.

The films provoked violence from its patrons. A cashier was pistol whipped for being rude to a customer. An usher was badly slashed in the thigh when he attempted to roust a drunken patron. Fights between customers were commonplace, sometimes fueled by the plethora of dangerous drugs peddled in alleyways and alcoves in shuttered store fronts. A woman patron was raped in the closed off balcony section. But the last film ever to run there, caused a final act of mayhem that closed the place for good. That film was Butchers of the Damned. A brutal, amateurishly shot gorefest, the film centered on an insane killer wearing a fright mask and using a hatchet and fillet knife on his victims. The film had been held over for two weeks. The same people would watch it over and over again, some staying for repeat viewings. Then the unthinkable happened,

According to management, this one guy had been coming back every night. That should have set off alarm bells, but it didn't. At the midnight showing on Friday night this guy walked over to the glass window where the firehose was kept. There was also a fire axe there. With everyone's attention focused toward on-screen carnage, no one noticed the guy. He took the axe out of the case, walked behind a patron, and cleaved his head in half right down to his shoulders. Then he ran out, he was never caught. The theater shut down the next day.

It was put on the market for sale and had no takers. Boarded up, it sat there for fifteen years, then fell into my hands. You see, my name is Dave, and I'm a realtor. My company saw potential in this property, but I didn't. It was on a block that was still decaying. Junkies, alkies, and the homeless littered the area. It would be a hard sell at best. I had someone interested, so I got the keys to the place and had the client meet me there.

The client was a fat, obnoxious man, Stan Blowstein, and he had his equally obnoxious son, Tommy, with him. Oh, Stan had plans as big as he was, but I already tuned him out. Heard it all before. I opened the door to the place, and it radiated cold. Considering it was summertime, I started to wonder how long it had been since someone checked this place.

There was about an inch of dust on the glass top of the candy counter. Rat gnawed old boxes remained. I saw all this, plus rats scuttling about as I turned the lights on. Motes of dust drifted though the dimness. "Ok if I look around," asked Stan.

"Yeah," I said, "but be careful." Tommy kicked over a rotting seat and laughed.

He went to kick another one then I said, "Please don't do that." He did it anyway and gave me a fuck you look.

"Stan," I said, "I just asked your kid not to do that, you want to take him out of here?"

"Oh, what's the harm," he bellowed with a laugh. "Place is falling apart anyway."

"That may be the case," I shot back, "But right now I'm responsible, so either he stops breaking stuff, or you can leave".

Stan wasn't the kind of guy who took any shit, but he rubbed me the wrong way from the get-go. He gave me a look which prompted me to say, "Ok, let's go."

Tommy now had gone somewhere in the building and returned wearing a fright mask and carrying a plastic axe and knife. These were advertising props for that fucking movie. "Put that stuff back where you found it," I yelled at him.

"No," the little bastard screamed back "Daddy, I want these."

"What's the harm in Tommy keeping these," Stan asked me.

"The harm is you're not here for a garage sale and that stuff isn't yours, mine or his. Are you interested in this building, or just what you can haul out of it?" My patience has come to an end.

"I want another agent," Stan bellowed, "Not a prick like you."

Fine I thought, gloves were off. "Ok, not a problem, have your brat put that stuff back and get out." Stan turned red and told me to go fuck myself. He left with the kid and the props, pretty much daring me to chase him down. Fuck him, his kid and that junk, I thought. I just wanted to be done with it. I figure maybe I better check the rest of this place before I leave.

Nothing seemed out of the ordinary. Then I checked the orchestra pit. There were several piles of what appeared to be bedding. Looking closer, I saw a couple of sleeping bags. But everything looked like it had been either clawed at or chewed. The stuff had brownish stains on it, maybe the pipes had leaked. When I looked closer, I saw what it really was, dried blood. I left quick.

I called the office and got chewed out about being rude to Mr. Blowstein. Then I told my side of it, finishing with, "his rotten kid stole stuff right in front of me."

"Well," my boss said, "You're out of it now."

"Thanks for small favors, and thanks for having the power turned on so I didn't break my neck in the dark."

My boss was silent for a minute. "Dave," he said slowly, "I didn't have the power turned on, what are you talking about?"

"Nothing," I blurted out, "Long tiring day, just tired and mumbling. I'll see you tomorrow."

Now I'm questioning my sanity because I know I turned those lights on.

There was a nasty adult bookstore, Blackjack Books, close to the theater. I thought that maybe someone working there knew something. The night manager was a surly thug known as Tondawanda Pete. He was an unshaven biker looking guy with a bandana wrapped around his head and a perpetual scowl. I approached the counter and he glared at me.

"Information isn't free here, pal," I was quickly told.

"Didn't think it was," I replied slipping a ten spot across the counter. "What do you know about the Liberty?"

"I know to stay the fuck out of the place," he said. "It was bad news the last two years it was open, now it's worse."

"How could it be worse if it's closed," I asked.

"People go in and don't come out," he said. "I'm here all night, around 4am, when its quiet here, weird noises come from inside that place."

"What kind of noises," I asked.

"Creepy fuckin' shit," Pete said. "Moaning, people talking, and a scream now and then. There were two big niggers that came in here, real tough bastards from Topp's Bar. They were going to rip the copper pipes out and scrap them. They broke in, but never came out. Do yourself a favor," he said. "Stay out of there." He went back to reading an issue of Screw.

Now I was curious as something was off here. I decided to go back and check something out. With all these derelicts in the area, some of them must have gotten into the theater to crash. It wouldn't be that hard to break into because no one would even report it. I was about to go through an alley to check an exit door, when I heard a voice say, "Don't go in there." The voice belonged to a big, dirty guy. He was about six feet tall, bearded with beady bloodshot eyes.

"Excuse me," I said. He looked me over like a cat looks at a mouse.

"You go in there, you die," he muttered.

"Really," I replied, "And you know this how?"

"The fuckin place is evil," he croaked, "really evil."

"All that shit they used to show there, the murders and shit, it made the place evil, like it absorbed all the bad shit and it stayed there." He looked me straight in the eye. "I had amigos that went in there to get out of the cold, I never seen them again. None of us go near the place, no matter how shitty it gets out here." That place will suck out your soul." I gave the guy a couple of bucks to grab a meal. Bullshit, I thought. A 'possessed theater'. Then I thought about the piles of bloody rags I found. A wrecking ball might be in order. It was getting late, and you did not want to be in this area after dark. I went home, made dinner, then turned on the news. There had been a gruesome murder the night before. A 30-year-old teacher had been found skinned in her apartment. I didn't give it much thought until a couple of days later.

A boy from the same school as the teacher was found in his backyard, dead. His head had been cleaved in half. Someone was seen running away. He was described as wearing a Halloween mask. "No," I thought, "that can't be possible". I decided to check something out. I called in a favor, I wanted to know where Tommy Blowstein went to school. I got more than I bargained for. Tommy was a 'problem child', and he had been threatening his social studies teacher who was just found dead.

He had also been picked on by a certain bully who was killed in his back yard. Now I was convinced something really fucked up was going on, but who would believe me. Three days later, Tommy Blowstein's gym teacher was attacked by someone wearing a fright mask and swinging a hatchet. He was badly cut up but managed to get away. His description of his attacker was really a description of the mask he wore and the axe he used. That description was of the mask the little bastard stole from The Liberty.

I went to the police. They weren't buying it. I said, "I wouldn't believe it either if someone told it to me, but just for shits and giggles, let's go with that Blowstein and his kid did steal that stuff right in front of me and I want it back." They sent a detective with me to get the crap back. We drove to Blowstein's address. The place was dark, not a good sign. As we approached the front door, I smelt rotting meat. The Detective, Mike, looked at me and nodded. No one answered the door, so Mike kicked it in. Stan had been tied to his recliner. He had been skinned and disemboweled. Parts of Mrs. Blowstein were scattered around the room. The incessant buzzing of flies almost masked the sound of Tommy attacking. The axe just missed my head, I was within an inch of getting my skull cleaved.

Tommy's near miss made him stumble. Mike dove onto his back as he tried to get up from the floor. "Pull that mask off him," I yelled.

The kid was bucking like a bronco; his strength was unnatural. Mike finally got his fingers under the mask and pulled. Tommy's face came off with the mask. Tommy let out a horrific scream. Eyes bulging out of a bloody skull face, he picked up the axe and went for Mike. Mike pulled out his service revolver. "Drop the weapon and get back," Mike yelled. The Tommy thing snarled and rushed at him. Mike shot him three times before he went down. Thick, red mist poured out of the wounds. Then it dissipated. Butchers of the Damned had claimed another victim.

There was an inquiry and there were no answers. I suggested to the police that maybe it would be wise to put those props back. I quit the area soon after that. I don't know if the Liberty is still standing. I still have nightmares about it. The building was a monument to evil and I hope someone had the sense to destroy it.

• • • •

The Liberty was a real theater in the middle of 42nd Street. It ran a lot of violent films including Caligula, which ran for almost four months.
Another favorite was Make Them Die Slowly that ran for ten straight weeks and was brought back a few times. It closed around the early 90's.

THE AMATEURS

On 'The Deuce' everyone has a hustle. But certain lines are set in stone, you don't cross them. You do, you pay a price. Sometimes people get stupid. You cross the wrong people; you get crossed out. This is a partially true story of two guys who thought they could buck the system.
There are certain people you don't lend money to. Period.

• • • •

IT WAS EARLY IN THE day at Club 44 on 44th street. An older man was having coffee with Candy, one of the bar maids. The man was called Father Tom. He chain-smoked Marlboro reds down to the filters. His fingers were stained yellow with nicotine. He was supposedly a former priest who left the church. He hung out in several dives and was tolerated. People didn't do business with him as his older brother had some real pull in the city.

For whatever reason, Father Tom was looking to borrow some money. Word went out to the local 'money lenders', don't, do not get involved with this guy. He won't be able to pay the vig and if the guy was pushed, he'd run to his brother. George 'The Hump' Castellano was the go-to guy for loans. He was called the Hump because he liked breaking people's 'hump'. in other words, he was a ball buster, a joker, but don't cross him. At 6' 2" and 250 pounds, he was a craggy faced bastard with salt and pepper hair.

The Hump would wander from bar to peepshow to whatever collecting what he was owed. You were light once; you got a warning to settle up. You couldn't settle up, you got something broken. The Hump walked into Club 44 and spoke briefly to Nino, the bouncer.

Father Tom approached The Hump. "Whatever it is, no," he barked at Tom. Tom retreated to his stool and lit another Marlboro off a dying one. Nino just shook his head. George gave him a wink and left.

Nino looked at Tom. "You no should bother the Hump, he won't do business wit you."

"I'll find someone, he isn't the only game here." Nino just walked away shaking his head. He had heard that Father Tom was a regular at The Show Place on 8th Avenue, a gay peep emporium. Nino didn't want the guy around his place, but like other places, he tolerated him until he got stupid. Stupid meant that Tom got drunk, chatty, and touchy feely. Nino would escort him to the door. Two semi regulars, Nails Morgan and Cueball Jones came into the bar. Nails was a big, white guy with a scarred face. Jones was an athletic black dude who dressed well.

Nino glared at them. "Didn't I 86 you last week?"

"Yeah, I think you did, but we come to settle up, no problems," Nails replied.

"Nino, my man, we had a little stroke of luck and had a good payday, we want to payoff our tab and buy you a drink," Jones added.

Nino went to the register and took out some slips of paper. "Dis payday, did it have anything at do with a building burning down in Chinatown?"

"No," Jones said too quickly. "We just picked up some muscle work from a friend who needed a little help."

Nino rolled his eyes, then gave them a total. Jones peeled off some bills, then put a fifty on top.

"For you, my friend, for putting up with our shit.:

Nino smiled and pocketed the fifty. "We be straight now, bruthers, tanks for the tip." The three men shook hands and parted.

"Where next," Nails asked.

"McGirr's, we need to settle up with Pop."

McGirr's was a huge pool hall. It had a snack bar with a surly old timer as a cook. He was called Pop. He saw Nails and Jones coming in.

"Your credit is shot, boys," he told them.

"Now wait, my good man, we are flush and want to settle up with this wonderful emporium," Nails told him

"It's 12:30, you guys drunk already?"

"Pop, we just got paid for a job and want to settle up."

"And we ain't been drinkin' either."

Pop pulled a couple of pieces of paper out of the register.

"You owe $38.50."

Nails peeled off a fifty and put another fifty on it.

"That's for putting up with us," Nails explained.

Pop shot him a hard look, then put all the money in the register.

"You're not taking that 50?"

Pop looked at them. "Ok, you're flush now, but how long before you're not? Look boys, I appreciate it, but I don't need it. I know you two, we ain't exactly friends, but yous are ok in my book. Comes a time when you're not flush, well, you're covered."

"Thanks, man, appreciate it, let's have a couple of burgers with fries," Nails said.

Rick McGraw and Bobby Ellis sat in a booth at Club 44 nursing their first beer of the day. McGraw was a short guy with red hair and a face full of freckles. Ellis was thin and wiry, about six foot and had thick black hair. The two were low level pot dealers that sold to students at The New York Institute of Fashion Technology. They had a steady, sort of no risk business going on. As a result, they usually had cash, but they, as most crooks are, looking to make more. McGraw was the more ambitious of the two. He admired the wise guys in the area and wanted to be like them.

"I need to get into something better than this nickel dime shit," he said to his partner.

Ellis took a swig of his beer and glared at him across the table.

"We do alright here, and we don't kick anything upstairs, we stay low keyed, and we do alright, you want more than that?"

"Yeah, I do I need to make more and get some respect."

"I'll take money over respect any day."

"Well, that's on you, I want better."

Ellis just drank his beer.

Father Tom came in smelling like an ash tray. He started chatting with the bar maids. He saw the two and wandered over to their booth. "Maybe one of you could help me out," he asked. The two didn't know Father Tom, nor did they know not to deal with him. McGraw was greedy and ambitious.

"What do you need help with," McGraw asked.

"I Need $200."

"Don't we all."

"I'm serious, it's Monday, come Friday, I'll give you $300."

That really got McGraw's attention. His wheels started turning. "Maybe I can help, let me go talk to a guy, I'll be back in an hour or so."

McGraw left, Ellis muttered, "fuck," and went after him.

"Rick, what the fuck are you doing? You're not going to deal with that asshole, are you?"

"It's my chance to make a score."

"So who is this guy you're going to see?"

"I'm not seeing anyone, I want him to think I am, that way I'm just the go in between. I'm gonna use my stash and make a quick C-note."

"You're going to get burned, that guy is a creepy little faggot."

"Did I ask you to get involved? I don't recall if I did, but this deal is mine."

"Fine, motherfucker, don't say I didn't warn you." Ellis stormed off.

McGraw went back to Club 44. Father Tom was nervously waiting. McGraw motioned for him to come outside. "I talked to my guy, and he said okay." McGraw gave him five twenties and two fifties. I'll see you here at noon Friday to collect," McGraw told him.

"Thank you so much, I'll be here then." Tom gushed.

Nino had noticed the exchange. He didn't like Rick as he was too mouthy. Nino made a phone call.

Ellis had wandered around before going to McGirr's. He sat at the counter, nodding to Nails and Jones. He ordered the meatloaf sandwich.

"You're one brave fucker," Nails laughed. "Who knows what Pop hid in there."

Pop turned from working the grill.

"When you learn how to cook, then critique my chow you idiot."

Nails just smiled at him.

"Where's your sidekick today," Jones asked.

"Doing something that I warned him not to do," Ellis replied. "You're pissed, I can tell."

"I am pissed, he's becoming more of an asshole every day. He just lent money to Father Tom."

"Is he nuts?"

"No just fuckin greedy and he thinks who he is, he wants to be one of the boys."

"Good luck with that if The Hump finds out."

Pop had been listening and chimed in.

"Did you hear about Hump and the lottery," he asked.

"No," Nails said, "did he hit it big?"

Pop laughed. "You know how George likes to break balls, right? He was in Gino's place collecting and Gino has a lottery machine. A lady came in to play this number, 1043. George hears her and goes into his act. 1043? Oh my God, I dreamt that number last night, I'm going to play it ten times, you should too."

Pop continues, "So the lady plays it ten times. She leaves, so Gino asks George if he wants 1043 ten times. Seems George was just being a fuckin ball breaker, but the fuckin number came out, it paid close to three grand. George almost shit himself when he found out."

"So that lady got like what, thirty-grand on a ten-dollar bet," Nails asked.

"Probably more, but The Hump just laughed it off," Pop said.

Jones looked at Ellis. "Might be time to find a new partner."

"I'll just see how far this crap goes, Rick wants to be a wise guy, that's his problem, I just want to earn a fuckin living with no hassles."

"Don't we all, Bro, don't we all."

Rick went into Club 44 at 11:45am. He sat at the bar and started chatting up Lisa, the sole barmaid on duty. Nino had a pretty good idea why McGraw was there. "Stop bothering Lisa and buy yourself a drink," he ordered.

"I don't want a drink, I'm waiting..."

"Then wait outside if you're not drinking, this is not your office."

McGraw seriously wanted to tell Nino to go fuck himself, but just glared at him. He ordered a bottle of Michelob so he wouldn't be kicked out. At about 12:05pm, Father Tom came in. He slipped McGraw a wad of bills.

"Here's the money as promised," but then he held it back. "If you let me hold this, I'll give you $500 next Friday."

"Are you serious?"

"Yes, I kept my word, right? I told you I'd have $300, and you see that I do, so why not trust me and make some more cash?"

A smarter man would have taken the $300 and called it a day, a greedy man wouldn't. Problem was that McGraw was very greedy and thought that he finally found his niche. He agreed to the deal.

Father Tom went to an apartment on West 46th Street where he scored two eight balls. He then went to the Show Place and watched the male strippers. Blasted on coke, he stuffed dollar bills into a young, Puerto Rican dancer's thong. After his set, he offered to buy the boy a drink. He and the boy went to a short stay hotel, the Dixie. The 'short stay' turned into two days of drugs and perversion. The kid left with a pocket full of cash. Father Tom was now broke.

By Wednesday Father Tom was sweating it out. No way could he come up with $500 by Friday. He knew he was in trouble but thought he could baffle Rick with bullshit. Friday came around and so did Rick.

Rick was at the bar when Tom told him that he didn't have the cash. "Give me another week and I'll give you $1000," Tom begged.

"You swore that you would have the bread today, I should beat your dumb ass for lying to me."

"I swear on my mother that I'll have $1000 for you next Friday."

"You damn well better, or I'll have your ass," snarled Rick. Father Tom scurried out of the bar. Rick finished his drink and left.

Nino had heard the entire exchange and made a phone call. "I need to see you," he said, then hung up.

About an hour later the Hump, himself, walked into Club 44. Nino took him into the back and told him what he had seen and heard. "Another candy store gangster, just what I need," The Hump stated. "He tinks who he is, even his partner walked on him."

"Who is his partner?"

"A guy named Ellis, he's ok, dey just deal a little smoke to the college kids."

"Tell him that I want to see him, no trouble, just a few words. Send him over to Gino's place."

"Ok, George, as soon as I see him, I'll pass da word."

Ellis walked into club 44 a couple of hours later. When he got the word, he was less than thrilled.

"I knew that greedy motherfucker would fuck me," Ellis bitched to Nino.

"No man, go talk to da Hump, he isn't angry wit you, he just wants to talk about your partna," Nino explained to him.

Ellis hustled his way to Gino's Place, where The Hump held council. Gino, a tall thin, balding guy in his early fifties, pointed to a door that led to a back room. Why do I feel like I'm walking my last mile, Ellis thought.

The Hump motioned to a chair. "Want something to drink, coffee, beer," George asked.

"No thank you, I'm good. I'm guessing this is about Rick?"

"Yeah, this is about your partner or am I wrong?"

"About the partner crap, yeah, I walked when he started what you want to talk to me about."

"I guess you're not that ambitious."

"How about I'm not stupid? I like money just as much as the next guy, but I try not to cross lines that aren't supposed to be crossed."

"Very astute of you, and that tells me you're a stand-up guy. What did your partner do with Father Tom?"

Ellis told him all he knew. "So, the good father is setting the vig and your boy keeps giving him cash."

"Yeah, Father Tom gave him $100 on $200, when I saw that, I walked. I told Rick this would blow up in his face."

"It's going to do more than that. The word was out not to deal with him, period. His brother has stroke and eventually will intervene when Tom can't pay. It won't be a kind intervention; your buddy will be in a jackpot."

"And me?"

"Keep your distance, divorce yourself, and just do what you have been doing. We aren't interested in nickel/dime hustles, but if you really want to earn, come and see me."

"Thank you, I will." The two shook hands and Ellis left. Outside, he breathed a sigh of relief.

Friday came and went. Seething, McGraw went looking for him. There was a kiosk on the corner of 42nd and 8th, run by a big guy of middle eastern decent called Blue. McGraw asked Blue if he had seen Father Tom.

"That ex-priest faggot? That's who you're looking for," asked Blue.

"Yeah," said McGraw, "he owes me some bread." "Try the Show Place, his 'boyfriend' dances there."

The Show Place was the gay equivalent of Show World, which was right across the street. The Show Place even had a complimentary buffet for its patrons. McGraw loathed to be seen entering the place, but he did. He foregoes the buffet and looks for Tom. He sees Tom sitting close to the stage with a dancer's crotch in his face. McGraw sits behind him, then slaps his head hard.

"Guess you forgot me, right, you piece of shit, where's my fuckin money," McGraw screamed in his face.

"I'm sorry," Tom cried, tears running down his face, "I'm really sorry."

"Fuck you and your being sorry, I'm going to take you out the back and beat the shit out of you."

"No, don't, please don't."

"Then give me the grand you promised me."

"I don't have it, I'll give you $1500 Friday, I swear."

"You swore you would have it today, and you didn't, I should just sell the debt to The Hump." Rick knew that was a complete bluff, but it scared Tom even more.

Shaking in total fear, Tom told McGraw to be at McGirr's tomorrow at noon and he would pay him $1500. "You fuckin better show up, pal." McGraw spit in his face, then left.

McGraw was at McGirr's before noon. He nursed a cup of coffee as he waited. A little after noon a well-dressed man entered McGirr's. He asked Pop about someone named Rick. Pop pointed to McGraw. The man approached Rick. "You have been lending my brother, Tom, money at a very high rate of interest. This stops now."

"Hey," replied Rick, "I just hooked him up with a guy I know, Tom was the one who set the rate."

"Well call your guy so I can settle up with him."

"It don't work like that."

"Oh, really? Well, here's how it's going to work; I write you out a check for $1500 and you stay away from Tom."

"I can't take a check."

"Then you're not getting paid."

"I need cash."

"Listen to me, you little punk, I'm giving you an easy way out." The man left a check on the counter for $1500 with no name on it.

"This ends it, kid, you try for more, you'll regret it," The man walked out. Rick picked up the check. He went looking for Ellis. Ellis was at Club 44.

"I need a favor," Rick asked Ellis. "I need you to cash this check."

"Fuck you, pal, seriously, fuck you."

"I'll give you a hundred for doing it." Nino walked over. "Buy a drink or leave now, stop bothering my customers."

"Bobby, I really need you to do this."

"Get the fuck out of my face."

Rick started to argue, then thought better about it. He slunk out of the bar.

"I'm going to see The Hump; I'm not getting jackpotted over this," Ellis said to Nino.

Ellis went to Gino's. "I need to see the boss," he told Gino.

"Wait here." Gino went into the back room. He came out and motioned Ellis to come in.

"You look pissed off," George said to Ellis.

"I'm beyond pissed off, you called it, big brother showed up and gave Rick a check. He wanted me to cash it."

"How big?"

"$1500, and the check just has the amount, no name on it."

"You see what's going on here? The minute your ex-friend puts his name on that check and cashes it, they got him. I want you to do something for me."

"Ok, what would that something be?"

"Tell him you can get that check cashed, then bring him here."

"Ok, then what happens?"

"You won't have to worry about shit coming back to you."

Ellis knew that McGraw won't be at Club 44, so he tried McGirr's. McGraw was trying to talk Nails Morgan into cashing the check. Nails told him that he didn't have a bank account. "Rick, come with me and I'll get that thing cashed," Ellis told him.

"Good, you finally got smart." Rick snickered. Ellis took him to Gino's.

"I got a guy here," Ellis told him.

Ellis ushered him into the back room. "Rick, meet George."

"You double crossing prick, I should..."

"You should know your fuckin place in life," George yelled at him. "Don't look at him, look at me because I'm the guy who you fucked."

"I didn't f..."

"Shut up, you're nothing here, so you're the smart guy that did business with someone who you never shoulda got involved with. By my estimate, you owe me $1300."

"I don't owe you shit." George got up and slapped Rick to the floor. "You involved yourself in my business, your $200 got you $1300 vig and that's my money, go cash that check."

"I can't, then he has me."

"Better him than me. Make up your mind."

"It's not fair."

"Oh, really?" George punched him in the face. Rick hit the floor, tears in his eyes.

"Not fair would be taking the whole thing, I'm leaving you your $200, you got an hour to settle up. Now go get my money."

McGraw was sobbing as he walked out the door.

"Bobby, you steer clear of that bum after he pays me but hang around until he gets back. If he ain't here in an hour, I'll need you to go find him."

"Fine, George, happy to help you end this shit."

McGraw went to the Chemical Bank. His hands were shaking when he endorsed the check.

"How do you want this," the clerk asked.

"Better make it all hundreds," McGraw told him.

McGraw toyed with the idea of hopping a bus for Jersey. He gave up that idea and went back to Gino's. George, Gino, and Ellis were talking about the Mets chances for the World Series this year. The phone rang and Gino answered. Gino listened, then handed the phone to George. "This is bad," Gino told him, "real bad." George listened for a couple of minutes, then told whoever was on the other end to stay where they are and wait.

George hung up, took a deep breath and explained the call. "Father Tom is dead in The Green Lantern Motel on 8th Avenue. He either overdosed or had a heart attack while he was getting his dick sucked. McGraw picked that moment to show up."

"You got my money," George asked him.

"Yeah, here it is." McGraw handed George the wad of bills.

"Now take off, I don't want to see you around here ever again." McGraw left. George turned to Ellis and handed him $300. "Go get yourself arrested," he told Ellis.

"Are you fuckin serious," Ellis asked.

"Kid, we have a mess here that we have to clean up. Your buddy is going down, and odds are, he'll talk. You'll get jackpotted, but if you're behind bars for something like a fight, being drunk, or pissing on a cop's shoes, you couldn't know anything about us cleaning up this mess. Whoever he was with is long gone, but you know they'll find drugs and the heat will be on."

"Don't worry, a night in the drunk tank won't kill you and I'll have you out tomorrow."

"And this money?"

"Consider it an advance, I can use a smart guy like you."

Ellis thanked him and left to get in trouble.

Rick McGraw awoke to someone pounding at his door. He answered it to find two detectives with a warrant for his arrest.

"What are you charging me with," McGraw asked.

"Extortion, maybe loan sharking and maybe murder. Your 'friend' Father Tom was found dead last night, now put your hands behind your back, we're taking you downtown."

• • • •

The lottery story is true. My father's store had a lottery machine. His friends would hang out and one was a guy named George who did tell a woman to play the number 10 times. He never played it; it did come out much to his chagrin. The money lending is also true, only the guy didn't die, his brother pit bulled the lender and he never saw a dime.

A CONFLICT OF INTEREST

From the late 60's to the end of the 80's, street prostitution flourished. Pimps 'recruited' by hanging out in bus terminals like Port Authority. They would check out who was leaving the buses that came in from the midwest. They looked for obvious runaways and 'befriended' them. This befriending could be getting them hooked on drugs or taking them to his place to be broke in. It was a scummy business, made even more scummy by the 'johns'. The customer could be worse than the pimp. Girls were beaten, tortured, and murdered back then. The cops didn't care because, hey, they are just a bunch of whores. But sometimes justice was handed down in the strangest of ways. Enemies become allies, the innocent are drawn into the loop, and justice becomes permanent.

• • • •

FRANK DENARDO WAS AT the bar in Club 45 nursing a Cutty and water. Frank was a hitman, and a good one. He only worked within the framework of the mob. No civilians, no torture, no prolonging the agony. If Frank got the contract, you were dead. Now, for the first time since he started his career, Frank was conflicted. He was contacted by Richie Colletti, son of Robert Colletti, a Capo in the Gambino Family.

Colletti wanted someone taken care of, but the target wasn't a wise guy, it was a working girl that pissed Richie off. He wanted her exclusively, but she didn't want him. Problem was that the kid had no class and came at her after too many cocktails. When she blew him off, he got loud and stupid. She slapped him in front of people. He went to punch her but her manager stepped between them. Now this punk wanted her dead and sidestepped his father to make it happen.

He contacted Frank, supposedly at his father's bequest. Frank knew this wasn't sanctioned and told the kid so. The kid got in Frank's face and told him, "You know who I am."

Frank's response was, "Tell your father to call me."

"I'll just tell him that you refused a personal favor, how do you like that, tough guy? You do what you're told." Frank just stared him down. He finished his drink and left.

Frank was about 6' 1", a bit stocky with thick black hair, a broad nose, and cold, blue eyes. He was a Vietnam Vet, doing two tours. He won a Silver Star and a Purple Heart. Frank was his own man and beholding to no one. This kid just put him in a jackpot. This girl who he wanted dead was called Jade. She was black, tall and a knockout. She wasn't a street walker; she was an expensive call girl. Even if he took the job, there would be dire repercussions.

Right now, prostitution was a black thing, but the mob smelled money and were trying to move in. When two black owned massage parlors opened, they started a price war. They were both firebombed during the night. The mob controlled the porn, the peeps, the bookstores and Star Distributors. Star shipped films, books and magazines all over the country. To say things were tense would be an understatement.

Up the block there was a place called The Wagon Wheel, a pimp bar. Willy was your stereotypical pimp: Fur coat, wide brimmed hat, gold chains etc. Darius was more subdued. He wore a three-piece suit. Willy was a big dude, 6' 4", and tough. Darius was about 5' 8", slim and neat.

They had a problem, one of their girls, Deidra, was missing for two days. Willie was pissed off. "If that bitch split on us, she's due for an ass whipping."

"I don't think she split," Darius said, "She was never a problem and always produced. No, something happened to her."

"Like something what? She gets into a car, sucks a dick, and she's done."

"I'm thinking she never got out of a car, that someone snatched her."

"Who'd be stupid enough to fuck with my property?"

"Someone who don't go by the rules, like one of those Jersey boys."

"You think one of those frat boys grabbed her?"

"Could be any of those cruisers. Look, they come over on weekends to score dope or pussy, you see all those Jersey plates around here on a Saturday night. Till we figure this out, warn the girls, no getting in a car with more than one trick."

Frank realized the position he was in. Richie was the apple of his Daddy's eye, next in line to take over. If jerk offs like Richie are the next batch of bosses, the outfit is in trouble, Frank thought. If I don't take the contract, the next one will be on me. Frank had considered leaving for over a year. He had a nice amount of cash stashed, enough to start over somewhere. Only he didn't think he'd need to make that move anytime soon. He needed to find this Jade girl.

Darius lingered in The Wagon Wheel. Willy went out to warn his stable. The bartender motioned to Darius. "Someone calling about a girl in the hospital." Darius grabbed the phone.

"This is Hackensack Medical Center calling. A woman was brought into the emergency room yesterday. She has been badly beaten and raped. She gave us this number."

"Give me your address and I'll be there shortly he told them."

Darius arrived at the hospital an hour or so later. He was met by a Lyndhurst Detective, Larry Winters. "Your friend was beaten almost to death. We found her in Lyndhurst by the dump. She has a broken arm, broken ribs, her front teeth have been knocked out and someone used her for an ashtray. Plus, she was raped and sodomized. My question to you is how did an obvious NYC streetwalker almost wind up dead in my town?"

"Detective, I don't know. Obviously, she picked the wrong john," Darius told him.

"More than obvious and I don't need this at my doorstep," Winters said. "She gave a description of these scumbags, but not a real good one. Two guys in their 20's picked her up in an old brown Caddy. One beat her while the other drove her across the river. What you do is your business, but this won't stand. I intend to bust these guys and I'll need her help. You need to watch for that fuckin Caddy if they try it again."

Darius agreed to let Winters know anything he could find out. He would also tell everyone to watch for that car. But Darius knew these guys would be back. They got away with it once, they would try again. But now he had information that he could use. A town, Lyndhurst, was only ten minutes outside the city. He knew a regular trick from there liked a particular girl, Ruby. Darius put the word out that he needed to talk to Ruby.

Ruby was a short, black girl with a big smile and even bigger tits. She met Darius outside The Wagon Wheel. "I need to talk to you about a certain john that's one of your regulars."

"Honey," Ruby said, "I gots a few regulars."

"This guy is from a town called Lyndhurst."

"Oh, that would be Chucky, he's a sweetheart."

"I need a word with him, when he shows up, bring him to me or let me know where you are."

"You ain't going to hurt him, are you?"

"No, but I need information, you know what happened to Deidra?"

"No, I don't."

"Two white boys put her in the hospital, I want those two."

"Sure Darius, I'll bring Chucky to you."

Frank made some inquiries as to where Jade worked. She was in an upscale spa, The Taj Mahal, a $100 house. He needed a word with her. The door man was a forty-something guy called Pug. Pug originally thought he got his nickname because he looked like a fighter, but he looked like the dog. His face was wrinkled and jowly, just like the dog. Plus, Pug always had the remains of an unlit cheap cigar in his mouth. "Never thought I'd see a guy like you paying for pussy," Pug said.

"In the overall scheme of things, we all pay for pussy in one way or another, don't we," Frank replied.

"No argument from me, you playing later tonight?" Pug was referring to a weekly card game held in the back of a smoke shop.

"Yeah, I'll be there to take your money again," Frank laughed. "I feel lucky tonight."

"Glad for you, I'm looking for a lady called Jade."

"Oh, think a black girl will change your luck?"

"Possibly, I'm sure she'll change something".

"I need a C-note, Frank." Frank gave him $100 bill.

"She's in suite A1, I'll buzz her, so she knows you're on the way."

Frank knocked on the door of the suite. It was answered by a tall, black woman with long, black hair. Her eyes were hazel, lips full and sensuous, in short, she was a knockout. "So, I was told your name is Frank, what is your pleasure, honey?"

"Right now, you and I need to have a conversation."

"Oh, you just want to talk. About what?"

"About keeping you alive, that's what."

Jade stiffened at that. "What the fuck are you talking about," she snarled.

"You had a slight problem with a guy named Richie Colletti. Seems you slapped him in public and now he wants to even things up."

"You're serious, aren't you?"

"Very much so, you see I'm who he hired, he wants you dead."

Jade went rigid and stared hard at him. "You'll never get away with it here," she told him.

"I'm not looking to get away with anything, I don't do civilians, women or children, but this kid jackpotted me with this. I have no intention of doing anything to you, but just because I won't doesn't mean that someone else won't take the job."

Jade sat on the edge of the bed and was quiet for a bit. She looked Frank in the eye. "So, what do you want to do?"

"I'm dead if I don't take you out, you're still going to wind up dead as they'll get someone else. Does anyone outside the outfit have your back, a manager or someone?"

"You mean do I have a pimp," Jade chuckled. "Yeah, I have someone."

"Can they get you out of town? Because that's the only option, I'll be leaving myself."

"My guy is called Darius; I think we both should go see him and see what he thinks."

"Ok, lets go see him, where does he hang out?"

"He's at The Wagon Wheel. I'll change and we'll go see him."

It took a lot of convincing, but Ruby got Chucky to talk to Darius. Chucky was a little bit scared. Ruby introduced Chucky to Darius.

"Have a seat, my man, what are you drinking?"

"A beer would be fine, thanks." Darius got Chucky a Heineken.

"Am I in some kind of trouble," Chucky asked.

"No, not at all, you be in a position to maybe help us straighten out a problem and get yourself some free trim in the process."

"What do I have to do?"

"Just give us some information, that town you live in, Liverworst."

"You mean Lyndhurst."

"Right, anyway someone from there drives an old brown Caddy and they fucked up one of the girls, we want those guys."

"Anthony Florie and Ritchie Polletti are who you want," Chucky told him.

"How the hell do you know this?"

"Because I hang out in the same bar that they do, and they were bragging about it. They are scumbags, you want a plate number? I can get it for you."

Darius looked kind of shocked. "Really?"

"Yeah, really, give me a number where I can call you. I really don't like those guys and I got sick after hearing what they did to that girl. I'll call you tomorrow."

"Ruby, take Chucky to your crib and give him a night he won't forget. Chucky, I will be expecting that call."

"I'll have it for you in day or so."

Jade took Frank to The Wagon Wheel. "Darius, meet Frank." Darius looked him over.

"Aren't you someone no one wants to see," Darius asked.

"Depends on the situation, and we do have a situation." Frank then explained everything.

When he finished, Darius looked at Jade and said, "Girl, you just had to smack that loud-mouthed wop, didn't you?"

"What did you expect me to do," she snarled. "Let him beat my ass?"

"No, you did right, but you did wrong at the same time. I take it this can't be fixed," he said to Frank.

"No, this punk dragged me into it, he's not about to back off, he even said I should consider this a "favor" for his old man."

"His old man is down with this shit?"

"More than likely not, but Richie is his heir and Richie wants what you have."

"We figured that after Marty, or someone burned those parlors," Darius said.

Just then, the bar phone rang. "Call for you, Darius, some white boy, Chucky." Darius excused himself and took the call.

"You have something for me?"

"Got a plate number and something else. The plate is ZKE 799."

"What's the something else?"

"They are going over there tonight."

"My man, you just scored you another night with Ruby."

Darius hung up and went back to the table. "Seems we may be in a situation where we could both benefit."

"How do you figure that," Frank asked.

"How would you not have to leave town?"

"I can't see how I can avoid leaving town."

"Well Jade has no choice, but you do. I have a situation where I need a favor."

"What situation would that be?"

Darius explained the problem. "I need these two gone, you need Richie gone, but you can't be the one to make him gone. We can."

Frank mulled it over. "Ok, how do we do this?"

"Jade has to go, Jade, were you wearing that pendant when you slapped Ritchie," Darius asked.

"I always wear this pendant," Jade answered. The pendant was a large gold cross.

"Ok, sorry, girl, you're gonna lose that and your hair."

"The fuck I am," she yelled.

"Cool down, bitch, it's your ass we are trying save here. You give Frank the pendant and some of the hair, he shows it to Richie and you're officially deceased. I'm getting you a bus ticket to Chicago, you'll be met and set up there. When shit calms down, I'll bring you back. Work for you?"

Jade thought for a minute. "Ok, I'll go get my hair cut and do what you say." She turned to Frank. "Thank you, I owe you and I pay my debts."

"Get your ass in gear, girl, Frank and I have to parlay a bit." Jade left.

"Shame you didn't get a piece of that for all this trouble," Darius said.

"She's sweet, but I'm more interested in keeping breathing about now."

Darius laughed. "I need you to hangout where my girls are and look for this brown Caddy with this plate number. When they start chatting up the girls, you get in the car and however you handle it is fine with us." Willy had come back and gave Frank a nasty look. Darius defused him.

"Frank is solving our problem, Bro, and we are going to solve his."

Willy nodded his approval. "After I take care of this problem, I'll be at the cigar store on West 46th playing cards in the back. You might want to cover that as I'm sure a certain party will be looking for me. I need a cold piece too."

Darius went to the bar and spoke to the bartender. The bartender went into a back room and came out with something wrapped in an oily rag. "This is as cold as Nixon's heart." It was a short barreled .38 revolver.

"Perfect," said Frank. He took a walk down to 9th avenue, a streetwalker hangout. He spotted Ruby. She saw him and nodded. Frank stood in a darkened alcove and waited.

Frank stood still as a stone pillar. His eyes watched the parade of cars checking out the inventory. A little after 11PM, a brown Caddy cruised the block. Ruby looked where Frank was waiting. Frank gave her a nod. The Caddy slowed up. Ruby went to the passenger window to discuss prices. While the two were distracted, Frank yanked open the back door, clubbed the passenger and held the gun to the driver's head.

"Drive," Frank ordered.

"Fuck you, you cocksucker, get the fu...." Frank pistol whipped him.

"I told you to drive, let's go, 12th Avenue down by the pier. People want to talk to you."

The passenger, Polletti, came to. "What the fuck is your problem, man?"

Frank stared at him, then spoke. "You like beating women, right, makes you a real tough guy?"

The driver, Florie, muttered "Hey, who gives a shit about a whore?"

Frank slapped the back of his head hard. "How about I do you, you fucking piece of shit. You think these girls like sucking Jersey jerk offs dicks? You think they enjoy this shitty life? Well, most don't, they are just trying to survive."

"Who gives a fuck, they are whores, they don't deserve anything except the $10 to blow me," Florie told him.

"Pull down to that warehouse," Frank ordered. They were at a rotting pier on the Hudson River. Transsexual hookers, drug burnouts, and bums prowled the area.

"So where is this nigger pimp you want us to see? Pretty fuckin bad that you're doing work for a nigger," Florie lectured him.

"You don't feel bad about putting that girl in the hospital," Frank asked.

"Fuck no, in fact we were hoping to do it again tonight, right Richie?"

Frank said nothing. He fired two shots though the driver's seat and two more though the passenger seat. Pieces of their hearts splattered the dashboard. Frank held two bullets in reserve. He checked; both were dead. He wiped down everything in the car, then the door. He broke down the gun and tossed the parts into the river. As he left, he saw shadowy shapes approaching the car. Within about twenty minutes anything usable will be taken. There will be so many prints on that car that it will look like a robbery that went south. He walked up to 9th avenue and hailed a cab. It was time to play cards.

"I think I'll stay open late tonight, with all the bars hopping, I might do some business," Murray said. Pug just showed up.

"Pug," George said, "How long has Joe Lewis been dead?"

"I don't know, a few years, I think," Pug replied.

"Then why do you still have his dick in your mouth," George asked. George cracked up. Pug scowled at him.

"Pug put that out I'll give you a good cigar, that thing smells light a horse turd," Murray told him.

"Wow," said George, "I should mark this day on my calendar, Murray gave out a free cigar."

"Are you burning trash in here," a new voice said. A slim Asian man entered the room, Mr. Lee. Lee had several takeout places and ran numbers on the side.

"Nah, it's just Pug's idea of fine tobacco," George replied.

"Fuck you people," muttered Pug, "I'm going outside."

"I think you hurt his feelings," Frank said.

"And you think I care?"

"Not a bit," laughed Frank. A slim Italian man walked in, he had hawk like features and eyes that didn't miss a thing. He called himself Mike Black.

"Pug seems a bit upset out there," Mike explained.

"We didn't exile him, but we let him know his smoke stinks," Frank said.

"Long as I know him, he always smoked cheap cigars."

"Cheap being the key word here," George added. "Let's get this game started."

The men took seats at the table "Let's start with five card stud," George announced.

Another man entered the store. Nails Morgan. "Is this a closed game or can I get a seat."

"Well as I live and breathe, Nails Morgan. Where's your sidekick tonight?"

"Jones has been seeing some lady."

"Is it serious?"

"I think if it goes another week, maybe wedding bells."

"Nails, this isn't a quarter, half and a dollar game, you sure you want in?"

"George, I'm kinda flush right now so I feel lucky."

"Good, the ante is $10 bucks." Everyone threw in $10. George dealt two cards down, then one up. Lee had a ten of hearts, Frank a seven of clubs, Pug, a ten of diamonds, Mike a Queen of Hearts, Nails an ace of clubs, Blue a five of diamonds and George a three of spades.

"Ace bets," George said.

"Make it $10," Nails said. The bet went to Mike, who raised it another $10. No one else raised until it came to Frank. "Make it $15." George dealt the next card. Lee got a nine of hearts, Frank got a jack of diamonds, Pug got a three of clubs, Mike drew a queen of diamonds, Nails drew a six of clubs, George drew a three of diamonds, Blue drew a five of spades. "Queens bet $20," Mike said, Nails met the bet, so did George, Frank raised another $20, Pug folded, Lee met the bet, George met the bet, Blue raised another $20.

George folded. "Got something good, you swarthy bastard," Blue chuckled.

"Good enough to beat that pair of threes you had," he replied.

Last card was dealt. Lee got a six of diamonds and folded, Mike drew a four of hearts, Nails drew a two of diamonds.

"Busted my flush, I'm out," he muttered, throwing his cards in. Blue drew a six of hearts.

"Queens bet," George said.

"Make it $50," Mike said,

"I see the $50 and raise it another $50, that's $100 to you, Blue," Frank said. Mike folded. Blue kicked in the hundred

"Calling you, Frank, whatcha got?"

Frank flipped over his cards, two sevens, the one up made it three.

Blue had three fives. "Son of a bitch, I thought you were bluffing," he said as he threw in his cards. Frank raked in the pot. Lee got the deal.

"Deal me a winner, you inscrutable bastard," George told him.

"Like the shit hand you just dealt me," Lee shot back.

"You know, I'll never forgive you for bombing Pearl Harbor," George told him. The boys cracked up.

"I never bomb anything, you dumb fuck, I sell take out," Lee admonished him.

"Just deal the fuckin cards, Lee," Nails told him.

"You one rude motherfucker, Nails."

"Blame it on my upbringing, I do," Nails laughed.

Lee just shrugged and dealt the next hand. Frank got an ace of hearts, Pug a four of diamonds, Mike a jack of diamonds, Nails an ace of spades, Blue a queen of hearts, George a nine of clubs. Lee dealt himself a king of diamonds, "First ace bets," George announced. Frank bet $20, when it got to Nails, he raised it to $20 more. Eyebrows raised.

"Got something good," Pug asked.

"It'll cost you to see it, Pug." Blue and George threw their bets into the pot.

Second card was dealt. Frank got a four of spades, Pug got a ten of diamonds, Mike drew a jack of hearts, Nails drew a queen of spades, Blue got a two of clubs, George got a nine of hearts, Lee got a seven of hearts.

"Jacks bet," George said.

"Make it fifty," Mike said. Nails matched it, Blue matched it, George matched it, Lee and Frank stayed in. Pug looked at his cards.

"You deal a hand like a foot," he told Lee, throwing his hand in.

"Fuck you GI, me love you long time," Lee said.

Everyone cracked up. Last card was dealt. Frank got a three of spades and folded. Mike drew a six of spades, Nails drew a jack of spades, Blue got a two of hearts and folded. "I'm beat on the boards here," he said. George got a nine of spades.

George was the bet. "Make it a hundred," he said.

"I'm making it two hundred." Mike bet.

"Make it three hundred," Nails said.

"You goofy fuck, what could you possibly have," asked Mike.

"Cost you to find out, Mike."

"Ok, I raise you another hundred."

"Make it two hundred and I call," said George.

Nails and Mike anted up. "Whatcha got, big guy," Nails asked. "What you see, three nines."

"Not good enough." Mike flipped over his cards. One was a jack of clubs. Everyone looked at Nails. Nails flipped over his cards, two aces.

"How the fuck ...," Mike sputtered. "You got me there, Nails, I never would have guessed." Nails raked in a rather substantial pot.

The deal was passed to Frank. Before he could shuffle the cards, there was a commotion in the storefront. "Where is that fuckin Frank," a familiar voice yelled. Richie Colletti. Colletti stormed into the room.

He was wearing a purple velour jogging suit and a lot of gold chains. He was pissed off. "Hey asshole," he addressed Frank, "didn't I give you a job to do?"

Before Frank could answer George cut in. "Private game, kid, you weren't invited."

"Fuck you, hump, in fact, fuck all of you. I'll be in charge real soon and shit's going to change."

Nails started to get up. "Nice suit, what happened to the nigger you stole it from?"

Richie's face turned beat red. "You're gonna pay for that crack, you ugly fuck." Nails grinned and got up.

Frank grabbed his arm. "Cool it, his beef is with me."

Frank reached into his pocket and took out a plastic bag with the pendant and a lock of Jade's hair in it. "Here you go, she's history."

Ritchie looked at the bag. "You think I'm buying this, where's the body?"

"You can't be that stupid that you would think that I'd whack someone and keep a body around for you to see?"

"Did you fuck her up like I told you too?"

Frank got up and got in his face. "You wanted her gone, she's gone. Case closed."

"No Goomba, it's not. I don't trust you one bit."

"Richie, I'm at the point where I don't care what you want," Frank snarled at him.

George now had all he could take. "Richie, you're a punk, look at you, you dress like a pimp. Then you come into my game making threats? There's the fuckin door, use it."

"You talk to me like that," Richie spat. "You forget who I am."

Now Mike chimed in "I know your father, he's a made guy, but then so am I. You're not fit to shine his shoes or mine. Does he even know what you're doing?"

"Fuck you too, Mike fuckin Black, can't even use your real name? He doesn't have to know what I'm doing, I'm gonna be in charge and I'll do shit my way."

"Go home, kid, I'm past the point of being annoyed, get out or I'll throw you out," George told him. Right now, Richie had three really pissed off bad guys in his face. He punked out.

"Ok, you old bastards play your game, I'll be talking to my old man and then maybe you'll get the idea." Richie flipped them a middle finger, then left.

"Talk about fucking up a fun evening, think he's going to tell daddy," George asked.

"George," Frank said, "Rest assured that he will, but I doubt anything will come of it."

"You think so, and what, pray tell, did you not do for him?"

"Something that is better left unsaid."

George just nodded. "Let's play cards."

After a few more hands, Pug dropped out. "They ain't running for me tonight," he muttered.

Murray handed Pug a cigar. "It's A Cuban, Pug, spit out that horse turd and try a real cigar."

"Well thanks, Murray, that really nice of you."

"Consider it a consolation prize."

"Pug, please take it outside and smoke it," Blue requested. "I don't know what smells worse, those cigars or Nails' dog's farts."

Everyone cracked up. "Fuck you guys, I'm getting some air." Pug went outside to smoke his stogie.

About ten minutes later Pug ran back in. "Something is going on down the block," he gasped, "lots of cops, squad cars and an ambulance."

"I'll go have a look," said Frank. "I'm coming with you."

"Ok, we'll take a break," said George. Frank and Pug walked down the block. There was a body of a guy in a blood-soaked purple jogging suit. Frank looked around and saw Willy standing in an alcove across the street. Frank gave him a little salute. Willy returned it and walked away.

"Another mugging gone bad," a detective said. Pug looked over the detective's shoulder.

"Not so tough, now, are you," he muttered.

"You know this guy," the detective asked Pug.

"Not really, seen him around, he had a lot of gold around his neck all the time."

"People never learn," the detective muttered. "You shouldn't wear gold around here. Ok, tag him and bag him," he ordered the paramedic.

Frank and Pug walked back to the store. "What happened," George asked.

"Someone mugged Richie and he's dead," Pug snorted.

"Someone was after all that gold he had around his neck. I guess he played tough with them, and they knifed him," Frank added.

"No great loss," Mike said. "I feel bad for his old man, but Richie was a jerk off."

"How about a few more hands, boys," asked George. "And hopefully no more interruptions."

"Yeah, why not? It's still early," said Mike. So, they played until dawn. Nails was the big winner. Frank felt he was the bigger winner. He saved two lives that night and one was his.

• • • •

The truth. Some scumbags did snatch hookers and beat them up. I knew two of them who did shit like that. Eventually the pimps found them and beat them half to death. Mike Black was a mobster who used to chat me up at Liquidators. I never knew his real name. Guys like Richie Colletti were 2nd generation mobsters who thought they were next to be the boss. Most wound up dead or in jail.

BUSTED

Club 45 was located on 45th street off 8th Avenue. It's claim to fame was that the run down bar was featured in two major movies, Midnight Cowboy (1969) and The Owl and the Pussycat (1970). The scene where Joe buck meets Ratso Rizzo was shot there. A huge sign in the window was there to let everyone know how cool this place was because of the films shot there.

• • • •

IT WAS AROUND 2PM AND two street guys were sitting at the bar. Del was a dark-haired man with a two-day growth of beard on his face and piercing blue eyes. He was wearing stained jeans, a sweatshirt that said Fun City on it and a watch cap. Larry was a bearded blonde-haired man wearing a long trench coat and a Mets ball cap. At a first glance, they looked like any bummer that infested the area. In reality, they were undercover vice cops.

    Larry had just come into the bar. He ordered a shot of old Crow with a Michelob chaser.

    "I don't know how you drink that crap," Del muttered, "it's one step above Ole Piss bourbon."

    "And what are you drinking," Larry inquired. "Cutty and water," Del replied.

    "Why not Johnny Walker? Cutty is on a par with Old Crow no matter how you look at it."

    "You'd be better served with Jack Daniels or go for the gusto with Maker's Mark."

    "Just what I need today, drinking tips from Del."

    "Have you heard anything about that creep, Bobby," Larry asked.

    "No, I know he's doing something with kids, and I want to nail his slimy ass to the wall, but no one is talking."

"This is dirty business, we nailed that one guy with the studio on 14th street for the dog films, shit makes me sick. In fact, this whole business disgusts me," Larry grumbled.

"I have been thinking a lot on this," Del said. "This is not going away, that movie, Deep Throat, is doing a lot of business. People want to see it, people are coming in from Jersey, Staten Island, even Connecticut, these fuckin peepshows are now tourist attractions. This is not going away."

"Ya know, maybe they should just make it legal, the regular fuck films, not this weird shit. It would make things easier for us, I mean I'm all for busting scumbags that fuck with kids, but if the other stuff was above ground...."

"We could actually bust guys committing real crimes," finished Del.

"We have busted Blackjack five times this week. They are open the next day. This fuckin city has had at least a dozen crackdowns in the last thirty years, has anything changed," Larry said.

"It's all nickel dime busts, nothing for the district attorney to sink his teeth in. We need a big bust, or we are just jerking off like the rest of these clowns," Del added.

McGirr's Poolroom on the corner of 45th Street and 8th Avenue was huge. Over two dozen tables, a snack bar and a regular bar. The 'No Cursing' sign had a couple of bullet holes in it. A thug known as 'Nails' Morgan was at the snack bar. Morgan had just been released from the hospital two days ago. Morgan liked to fight, his last brawl put him in the ER with broken ribs and a punctured lung. Morgan was deciding on his breakfast, or what he could afford for breakfast because he was broke.

"How much for an egg sandwich," he asked Pops, the cook.

"Can you read? The damn prices are right here." Pops points to a sign over the grill.

"Don't get testy, I just asked a question, I'm on a fuckin budget here. Ok, ninety-five cents for the egg, twenty-five cents for the coffee, how much for a beer?"

"A buck," Pop sourly replied.

"So that's two bucks and twenty cents, ok, serve it up."

"So much for a tip," Pops snickered.

Morgan slid him three singles, "Call this even."

Morgan was eating his breakfast when a tall black man with a shaved head joined him at the counter. Cueball Jones was his name.

"Nails, my man, when did you get out?"

"A couple of days ago, sucked being in there for like ten days."

"Yeah, those guys fucked you up good."

"Jonesy, I'm pissed, it was one on one with that big cocksucker, Dolls, then the other two had to jump in."

"Dolls just got out a couple of weeks ago, he's making a lot of noise around here."

"Yeah, like shaking down all these mutts in the bookstores. He wants a quarter a reel for every loop sold. He says that he will keep people from duplicating that stuff. What a crock of shit."

Morgan lit up a Marlboro Red.

"Didn't you just have a punctured lung," Jones asked.

"Yeah, the doctor said when he released me that I could go back to normal activities."

"Smoking cigarettes, drinking beer at 9am are normal activities?"

"They are now."

"What are you going to do about Dolls?'

"Nothing, let that wop cocksucker step on his own dick. He keeps pushing his shit and one of his own goombas will punch his ticket. He isn't acting on anyone's behalf, he's muscling his way in. Hell, I heard he threatened to kill Bobby's little dog."

"Bobby loves that dog."

"Yeah, that and money. Midtown Books has been packed since the last raid."

"Bobby is a fuckin weasel anyway. He'd sell you out for a nickel. Remember when they had him in court?"

"Yeah, he faked a heart attack. The cops had their own doctor check him. Then he had his appendix taken out. He did something with a doctor to make him keep having a high fever. Fucker did not want to do time."

"I hear he got real chummy with that vice cop, Joe something."

"Another reason to avoid that slimy little fuck."

Further conversation was interrupted when a huge man in a red jogging suit walked down the stairs and into McGirr's, Eddie Dolls. Jones looked at Morgan and said, "What the fuck does he want?"

"I'd guess it's me," replied Morgan, "Guess he wants to finish the job." "Hey asshole," Dolls said, "I see you're up and around."

"What's the difference between an Italian Grandmother and a baby elephant," Morgan asked.

Dolls looked perplexed.

"Fifty pounds and a black dress," Morgan finished.

Dolls face turned red. "Guess you need another ass whipping, big mouth."

"What, just you this time? Last time you needed two guys to hold me down."

"Hey, take that outside," Pops yelled, "No fighting allowed in here."

"Whose gonna stop me, old man, you?"

"No," Pops said. "Hey rube," he yelled.

Three bruisers had been playing pool. The stopped and surrounded Dolls, brandishing their pool cues.

"This shit don't fly in here," Pops snarled. "You ought to know that this is neutral territory."

"Who says so?"

"Sonny, that's who, you got a problem with that, take it up with him. Now hit the bricks."

"I won't forget this, you old bastard."

"Gee, I'll just cry me a river before I go to bed tonight." Dolls turned to Morgan, "I ain't done with you yet." Morgan just stared him down. Dolls stormed off.

"Better watch your back, man," Jones said.

"No shit, I wonder if the other wise guys know that this prick is moving in on them."

"If they don't, they will soon. Dolls ain't none too subtle about taking things over."

"From what I'm hearing," said Jones. "Dolls gets busted again; he won't see daylight for years."

"Ya know, Jonesy, I'd love to see that happen."

Del had gone back to the precinct to find out what to do next.

"Bust Blackjack's again," the captain told him. "I want Brochinni to make a mistake."

"Ok, Cap, I'm on it, again."

Del, Larry and a few uniforms go to Blackjack Books, a little shithole in the middle of the block. Live Sex Shows, The San Francisco Theater of S&M on the 2nd floor, male hustlers hanging outside waiting for tricks to blow them in a peep booth for $10, Blackjack's has something for everyone.

"Not again," groaned Tonawanda Pete, the manager.

"Hi Pete," Del said.

"You cocksuckers have no mercy, why can't you bust this fuckin place before or after my damn shift?"

"Truth is, we like you, Pete, you're the most personable guy here." Pete was a former Vietnam Veteran who did two tours and was pretty much soured on life. Pete was anything but 'personable'. He was 6' 3", 250 pounds of muscle and gristle with a three-day beard, and a bandana covering his head. Pete was notorious as he killed a guy who had cut him and tried to rob the store.

"You could at least order me a pizza, I'll be in The Tombs for another 24 hours and that slice of baloney on white bread sucks." Del motioned for Pete to step out from behind the counter. "Where's the animal films, Pete?"

"I have no idea what you're talking about, this is a family store," Pete snickered.

"So, we have to tear the place apart," Larry asked.

"It's your world, bro, I just live in it."

"Have it your way." Larry put the cuffs on him.

Pete just watched as they rousted patrons from the peep booths. Cueball Jones emerged from one.

"Hey Pete, busted again," Cueball asked.

"Yeah, another thrilling day in the company of New York's finest. How's your buddy Nails, healed up yet?"

"He's out and walking, what happened was bullshit. That fuckin Eddie Dolls starts something, then can't finish it. So, his goombas jump in. Nails isn't at 100%, far from it and this fuckin wop keeps pushing."

"He's pushing the wrong people," Pete said, "and they don't like being pushed."

"Later, bro," Jones said as he and others were shown the door.

A young, black teenager walks into the store with two large boxes on a hand truck.

"Fuck no," Pete muttered. "Hey Kid, we're closed, take a hike."

"Not so fast," ordered Del, "what do you have there, kid?"

"I'm jest makin' a delivery," the scared kid said.

"Well let's just see what you're delivering."

Del slices open one of the boxes. He pulls out a white box with an 8mm film in it. 'Dogarama' is stenciled on the box.

Del shows it to Pete.

"Nothing to do with me," he stammered.

"Really," asked Del. "You're the manager and yeah, it's here on your watch. Take him downtown," Del told one of the uniform cops. Del turned to the kid. "Tell me where you got this."

"I don't want to get in trouble," the kid said.

"You're already in trouble, the amount of trouble you're in could be lessened by cooperating."

"I'll lose my job, just look at the carton."

The label on the carton read Cinelabs 421 west 54th Street New York, NY.

"Bingo," said Larry, "fuckin bingo."

Del motioned Larry over. "I don't want to bust this kid, but I don't want him tipping these guys off either. He's just some poor shlup trying to make a living."

"So how do we do this," Larry asked.

"Ok, son," Del said to the Kid, "you're going to the movies." Del hands him a five spot. "Pick a double feature and stay there. If we find out you tipped off your bosses, you'll be joining them in the Tombs."

"I ain't sayin' nothing." The kid took the money and left.

Del and Larry had a squad car drive them to West 54th Street. Cinelabs was a film processing lab run by two middle aged Jewish men. Herbert and Sol. The two protested loudly as Del and Larry produced their badges. The lab processed industrial films, commercials, and porn, more porn than the two vice officers had ever seen before. Del asked for invoices, the two refused. They called their lawyer who got there in a New York minute.

Del made things simple, he told the lawyer that they will shut the lab down tighter than a clam's ass. "Just give us the invoices for the porn stuff and we won't shut you down or confiscate everything here." The lab owners and their lawyer had a hasty conference. Lots of shouting and hand waving. In the end, it was in their best interests to turn over the invoices, and the inventory of finished films.

The inventory was staggering, thousands of 8mm and 16mm films. Del had no idea of how to transport it. Larry was looking over the massive inventory.

"How the hell are we going to get all this trash out of here?"

The 'trash' comment gave Del an idea. He called the precinct and told the captain that he needed a garbage truck to come to Cinelabs address and send some officers over to help. It took ten hours to fill that truck and they had to send for another one.

Cue Ball Jones was walking down 42nd Street. He was by Midtown Books when he saw Bobby outside, talking loud to a guy Jones knew as a cop. He couldn't hear much, but he did hear Dolls and wiretap.

"So, this little bastard is a snitch," Jones muttered to himself.

Jones was close to a kiosk on the corner of 42nd and 8th Avenue. Nails was trying to make some kind of deal with Blue, the big middle eastern guy who either owned it or worked there. Blue was called Blue because he had 5 o'clock shadow at 10AM. That gave his rather large face a bluish tint.

Nails wanted a pack of Marlboros on the arm. "C'mon, Blue, I'm good for it," Nails whined.

"Yeah, you and everyone else on this block", Blue shot back.

"Give him the smokes", Cueball told Blue, "I'll pay for them."

Blue slid Nails a pack. "We gots to talk, man," Jones said to Nails.

They hung a right on 8th Avenue. Jones ducked into an alcove of a closed store. "Listen up," he said to Nails, "your problem might have just solved itself."

"Wadda mean, it solved itself?"

"I just overheard Bobby giving up Dolls, his cop buddy put a wiretap on him."

"And that fuckin dago loves to talk."

"Exactly, you should just lay low for a few days, see how this will all shake out."

Larry and Del were out with a couple of others celebrating what turned out to be a fruitful day. The invoices from Cinelabs had just about anyone who made loops in NYC and other places on a list. That list included several heavy hitters and mob guys.

"That was a home run, Del, what a break that Blackjacks got a delivery in the middle of a bust," Larry said.

"We pretty much got them all, Joe Bikini, Marty, Bobby, Helwig, even those S&M creeps that shoot films across the river."

"Do you think this is the end of it?"

"No, we just threw a roadblock in front of them. Give it a couple of weeks, a few convictions, and the circus starts all over again."

"Then we go back to fighting crime." The group toasted each other.

At another dive bar, Club 44 on 44th Street. Nails and Cueball were watching the news. A large man in a red track suit was being escorted out of a warehouse downtown.

"Isn't that Dolls," Cueball asked.

"Well fuck me, it sure is," replied Nails, "they finally got him."

"So, it's a great day for the forces of law and order in our fine city."

The two burst out laughing and toasted the fate of Eddie Dolls.

• • • •

Blackjack Books was owned by Joe Bronchinni aka Joe Bikini. The building was owned by Martin Hodas, the Poppa of the Peeps. Joe was murdered in his used car lot in an unsanctioned mob hit. Blackjack Books had a laundry list of obscenity and prostitution busts. It was one of the few peep places that never cleaned up its act. It had sawdust sprinkled on the floor, broken peep booths and a cruising scene in the booth area I believe it closed in the late 80's. McGirrs Pool Hall was one of the biggest pool halls in the city. Not sure if it's still open.
Cinelabs was a film processing lab that processed most of the NYC shot 8mm loops.

Eddie Dolls was a mob guy who did get busted in that wiretap but was let go due to insufficient evidence. That 25 cent 'tribute' per reel for 8mm loops is true. That was the price of doing business.
Bobby was Bobby Surretsky, a pornographer who owned Midtown Books. He did buddy up to a certain vice cop who eventually turned him into a snitch. He was also involved in a murder for hire plot. Not sure what became of him. I did meet him when I was younger as I frequented Midtown Books.
Larry and Del were based on undercover cops that prowled the area.
Tondawanda Pete, Nails Morgan and Cueball Jones were based on guys I ran into now and then on 42nd Street and at Club 44.
Those 'S&M creeps across the river' refers to a brand of films, RDF, which were shot in Jersey with real S&M aficionados.
The garbage truck story is real. After the Cinelab bust they used more trucks to clean out warehouses of films.

TERRIBLE TOM

Sitting at a counter at a luncheonette on West 43rd street, Terrible Tom was agitated. Tom was in his early 40's, balding with a bullet head, mustache and piercing brown eyes. It was said that he was cold enough to stand over a guy he put a hit out on, eating an apple. Tom was no one to cross, he kept order in his part of the world. His thing was moving stolen goods that had been hijacked from trucks and from the docks.

Right now, business was at a standstill because of a situation. The situation was that the Feds wanted Tom and others that he was involved with. They took a vicious junkie called Vince the Prince and made him their informant. Vince was five foot nothing, a weasel who carried a straight razor. The Feds had no idea what they were letting out. Vince was ambitious and assembled a crew of vicious assholes to back him up.

They started demanding protection money from local merchants. Broken windows and late-night fires happen frequently. Tom had money invested in some of these businesses, he was beyond pissed off. Something had to be done, but what? Vince was protected. If he did cross the line, he was bailed out by his 'handlers'. Tom was waiting on someone to discuss the problem. A slim, long-haired guy came in and took a seat next to Tom.

Gregory was a bank robber. He had robbed eight banks so far. He had a system. He walked in wearing a ski mask and coveralls. He carried a shotgun. He would fire the gun, clean out the tellers, then run into a wooded area near by. He had a change of clothes stashed. He would bury the cash, gun, and clothing, then come back weeks later to pick it up. Vince had been getting way too friendly with him. Gregory hated rats.

"So, things aren't good with you either," Gregory said to Tom.

"Things aren't good for anyone with this fuckin rat Vince breathing my air."

"Agreed, he keeps asking what my next move is, do I look that stupid?"

"These fuckin' feds, they do this all the time. A made guy wouldn't say anything, this fuckin' junkie would give up his own mother."

"What do you want to do about this, Tom?"

"He's got to go, no other way, and some of his crew too. You know he shot up a cab Saturday night and was bailed out?"

"Yeah, I know because I put up the bail money."

"Why the fuck did you do that?"

"Because I know what has to be done and I need to keep him off balance. He doesn't know that I bailed him out, I got there before the feds did."

"So, what's the plan," Gregory asked.

"First, we need a clean piece. I know where I can get one."

"Risky, aren't we being watched?"

"Not everyone, I know a guy who Vince jackpotted. He got scared and left the state. He came back a couple of weeks ago and got busted for weed. It's Pete the peddler, he's in panic mode right now, trying to sell off stuff to pay his lawyer. Rumor has it that he has a 9-millimeter he needs to get rid of. I'm going to pay him a visit. Are you in?"

"Yeah, I'm in, I can't get my work done with him hovering around here."

"Good, I'll pay Mr. Pete a visit."

Pete the Peddler was a skinny guy with long red hair and an unruly beard. He was a complete pot head and was paranoid. He was well known around the area. His business card read, 'Before You Buy Anything, Call Me'. Terrible Tom was the guy who gave Pete his start. Now he wanted a favor. Pete was at his rented garage, loading his van for a weekend of flea marketing. Tom pulled in behind his van.

"How was your New England vacation," Tom asked.

"A lot more peaceful that it is around here," Pete replied. "I heard you had a visit from The Prince."

"Wasn't a visit, the cocksucker held a gun to my head and cleaned me out. Then he accused me of narcing him out and I was supposed to give him more money. So, I booked."

"Then you come back and get busted for a couple of roaches in your ash tray?"

"And a sword, don't forget the fuckin sword. I had a price tag on it and that cop peeled it off, said I attacked him with it, lying fuckin prick."

"Did you get a lawyer?"

"With what? I haven't made squat since that asshole has been around and I got a public defender who wants me to cop a plea. I'm not coping a plea, that pig broke one of my fuckin taillights so he could pull me over."

"And how do you know this?"

"Because I just replaced those lights because I have to get this thing inspected, that's how."

"Maybe you should get a more discreet ride and not have your buddy paint skulls all over so he can try out his new paint sprayer."

"You know everything, don't you?"

"I know you have something that you shouldn't have, something you need to get rid of."

"Yeah, that fuckin gun, I don't need any more problems."

"So, I'll take it off your hands, it is clean right?"

"Yeah, no history, I bought something that was promised to someone else. He got real irate when he found out he got backdoored and I got it. I just wanted a piece and didn't need the hassle, so I traded that gun for the 9. $250 takes it."

"No, more like $150 and consider yourself lucky, it won't come back to you."

"Tom, I need the bread, I have to get my shit..."

"Remember who started you, Peter, remember who gave you credit so you could start this little thing of yours."

Pete looked very sheepish at this point. Tom continued.

"It was your choice to smoke weed, your choice to hang out with assholes, now look at the big picture, time to do the right thing for the greater good."

"I'm sorry, I do owe you a lot, I'm just all fucked up with this bust. Just take the damn gun, forget the money."

"Tell you what, I'll do you one better, I'll call my lawyer. You'll get something, but you won't do time."

"Thanks, Tom, now I'll tell you two things you don't know."

"What might those two things be?"

"Vince has an ear with one of the local cops, that's why he's so hard to pin down. And your friend, Steve, that big fuck, he's a rat."

"How do you know Steve is a rat?"

"Because he pistol whipped a guy who is related to a police chief. He folded up when he got locked up, he's been talking a lot, asking questions about who's doing what, that's how."

"I'm going to check this out. Before you leave, put that package in that box in front of garage #A1. And Pete..."

"Yeah?"

"We never saw each other today."

They shook hands and Tom drove off. Pete took something wrapped in an oily rag from under his driver's seat. He put it in the box, finished loading up and drove off for the weekend.

Tom drove over the George Washington Bridge to a town in New Jersey, Englewood. He had to see a man named Angelo, the real boss.

Angelo greeted Tom warmly and they settled in Angelo's den, sipping good scotch.

"So," Angelo asked, "do we have a solution to this problem?"

"Things have been set in motion," Tom replied, "I hired a plumber."

"You mean your friend, the bank robber?"

"Greg stepped up to the plate on this, I didn't have to ask."

"That kid has a big set of conjones on him. That last bank he hit was in The Willow brook Mall."

"Well, so far no one has made him yet"

"It's only a matter of time. Look, I know you like the kid, but he's an outlaw. Did you hear about his buying friends a Mexican lunch?"

"No, what was that about?"

"It's about how reckless he can be. He was with a couple of his friends, and they decided they wanted to eat Mexican. Greg flew them to Mexico for lunch. That's the kind of thing we don't need."

"We will owe the guy after this, kinda hard to tell him anything, remember how he handled Sgt. Muldoon?"

"Yes, and that was another situation. I know that cop is a scumbag, but shooting up his Caddy, then mailing him the gun with a note saying, 'Do we still have a problem?' was way over the top. Just sit him down after this and set him straight."

Tom knew better than to argue the point.

"Ok, when this is wrapped up, I'll have a man to man talk with him."

Tom was in his usual spot the next day. Greg came in, ordered a cup of coffee, then said to Tom, "I picked up the package."

"Good," said Tom. "Now we have to disconnect, call me when the job is done." Tom finished his coffee and left. Greg was thinking how this was going to play out. He knew Vince had a girl he shacked up with. Best thing would be to take him when he was leaving. He had never shot anyone before. He could do it, he thought, if he didn't, he was out of business.

Vince was out partying with his brother Nicky, Big Steve and a guy they called Danny Douche. "Pretty soon, boys, we will be running things", Vince told them.

"I don't like that you're talking to the feds," Nicky told him.

"It's the way to get things done, brother," Vince told him. "They really want Terrible Tom and I'm going to give him to them. Then we write our own ticket."

"I doubt that," Nicky replied.

"Don't question me, ever," Vince snarled back. "I have this".

Vince was fueled with heroin, his drug of choice. Unlike other addicts who just nodded out, the drug brought out the worst in Vince. A look or a comment would have a straight razor pulled on them. Vince sliced up a guy in a bar for just ignoring him. Nicky was an addict too, but he just followed his brother. Big Steve sold drugs to high school kids. He used his size to bully people. Danny the Douche, unbeknownst to Vince, was another rat. He reported back what Vince was doing. Danny played both sides. He would walk away from this and go into the witness protection program. Too stupid to stay away, he returned to the area and was stabbed to death in a cheap motel room. He had burned a couple of guys in a drug deal.

Greg had followed Vince to some girl's apartment. He weighed his options. If he burst in, he would have to kill the girl, something he didn't want to do. So, he waited. Vince left the apartment while Greg trailed him to a parking lot. Vince picked up a car and drove toward the Lincoln Tunnel. Greg hailed a cab and followed him to a small town across the river. Vince was parked in front of a small house.

Greg had the cab drive a couple of miles away to a bar. He got out and went into the bar. A few minutes after the cab left, Greg hoofed it to where Vince was. Greg climbed quietly onto the porch and looked through the window. Vince was sprawled on a couch, watching something on television. Greg took out the gun, he had nine bullets in it. He aimed though the window and fired.

The first shot hit Vince in the shoulder. He was up as two more shots zipped past him. A fourth bullet grazed his side, the next two hit him high and low as Greg was having trouble aiming. He fired two more shots and he missed. His last shot caught Vince under his arm.

Vince staggered out of the room. Greg took off, running toward the Passaic River.

Vince stumbled into a kitchen where his mother was cooking something. She looked at her son in horror as he slumped to the floor. "Ma, I'm scared," he muttered as he bled out on the floor. Greg made it to a bridge and started disassembling the gun. He tossed the parts into the river, then went to a pay phone.

Terrible Tom woke up to his phone ringing. He picked it up and a voice said, "This is your local plumber, I took care of that leak for you," then the phone went dead. The murder shook up the small town.

Nasty secrets were coming out as people started talking. The feds were questioning everyone but go no answers. One of Vince's victims was accused of going into New York and hiring a hit man. The guy in question wouldn't know a hit man if he tripped over one.

About a week later, Nicky was run over on Route 80. Seems he 'fell' out of a car. Big Steve continued to sell drugs. He was found dead in his car, someone made him eat his stash and chased it with a fifth of vodka. No one was talking as the feds questioned everyone. People were celebrating Vince's death. Eventually, the feds left the area, but had eyes on Greg.

Tom visited Angelo, who was pleased that the 'problem' had been resolved.

"Did you talk to your outlaw friend about laying low for a bit," Angelo asked.

"I did," replied Tom, "for all the good it will do."

"Tell that peddler guy to keep his pot smoking friends off the streets. We don't need any more heat here."

"Pete will listen to me, don't worry about that."

"Good, now we can all go back to work and just not be too obvious about things."

Well things went back to normal for a while. Nine was the charm as Greg got caught robbing his ninth bank. People kicked into a defense fund, but the Feds wanted the bank robbery, and Vince's murder, to stick. Problem was that they couldn't find the gun. Greg got 20 years in a federal prison. A prison that was a few stories underground. That prison was the future home of John Gotti.

Greg being Greg, there was an attempted breakout involving a helicopter. That went south quickly. Greg was going to do his last few years in another prison in Pennsylvania. He was stabbed to death in the chow line there. In a weird twist of fate, he was buried not far from the man he killed.

• • • •

This story is based on true incidents that happened in the mid 70's. The Feds were using scumbags as informants and this time it backfired.

WRONG PLACE, WRONG TIME

Every week the proceeds of sin were dropped off at Shelly's apartment. Quarters from the peepshows were taken to Chemical Bank and converted into bills. Those bills along with the weekly take from massage parlors were delivered to Shelly and then were picked up by an associate of DB. DB was the boss of Times Square. He controlled all the porn and vice in that area. Shelly owned a couple of porn theaters and was a trusted drop off point as no one would suspect that she had any money.

This week's take was larger than usual, over 25K. Marty's right hand man, the hulking Eddie Burns, dropped of the suitcase. "Better take good care of this," Eddie instructed Shelly. "Marty will have this picked up tomorrow." Shelly took the suitcase and put it in her room. Shelly was a lesbian in the Shelly Winters mode, a larger woman, very streetwise. She had a lithesome young blonde, Beth, sharing her place. Beth was a live show performer that Shelly discovered working at The Doll on 7th Avenue.

After the loot was dropped off, Shelly hid it under a bed. Two live sex show performers, Terry and Candy, stopped by to shoot the breeze. Terry was a hot Puerto Rican chic who did shows with her husband, Phil.

The two were big time coke heads who could screw all day. Phil's claim to fame was that his cum shot could hit the third row of patrons. Candy was a slim, black girl who was always in demand as a performer. Shelly didn't expect them. The two women laid out lines of blow.

Invited, Shelly backed off, but Beth did a couple of lines. The coke was superb and hadn't been stepped on. The girls were enjoying their buzz, then someone knocked on the door. Shelly answered it. The door flew open, and Shelly was knocked on her ass. Two men with ski masks forced their way in. Terry was up and in their faces until one slashed her throat with a straight razor.

Blood shot out of her neck in three-foot arcs. Candy tried to help her but was punched in the face and hit the floor. Her assailant grabbed her hair and cut her throat. The walls were splattered with blood and the floor was a river of it. One man grabbed Beth and screamed "Give us the fuckin money or we'll do her next." Shelly dragged the suitcase out from under the bed. One of the men grabbed it. "Here's your receipt," he said, then slashed Beth's face.

Shelly called the police. It was called a rampage murder. The headlines in The New York Post screamed: **Dancers Butchered, Drug Deal Goes Bad**.

No mention was made about the money, but those in the know realized that someone crossed a huge line. Shelly was questioned by the cops and the mob. She couldn't identify the men because of the masks. All she knew was they were white and crazy. Terry's husband, Phil, was brought in for questioning. Phil was devastated and pretty much a basket case. People who ran the business wanted these guys and put a bounty up.

Two unsavory mid-town detectives had the case. Morelli and Muldoon. Morelli was a slim Italian guy with an eye for the ladies. Muldoon was a burly Irishman with a bulbous nose from drinking. Morelli was the brains, Muldoon the muscle. Muldoon enjoyed beating on 'skells' as he knew they couldn't do anything about it. This case was a 'priority' for several reasons. One, the boys on 'the pad' didn't get theirs. Two, a rampage murder was terrible for business.

"We should check out every joint on the strip and see if anyone heard anything," Morelli told his partner.

"You think those guys would know anything," Muldoon asked.

"One never knows," said Morelli, "but let's look for someone dropping a lot of coin in the peeps and strip joints."

The Metropole and The Mardi Gras were two big strip joints on Broadway. A guy named Big George was the 'owner'. George was nursing a cup of coffee when the two detectives stopped in.

"Pretty quiet in here today, George," Morelli announced.

"Murder has a way of dampening people spirits," George told him. "Plus, some of the girls aren't coming in until you catch these guys."

"So, we take it you heard nothing", grunted Muldoon.

"No," replied George. "I wish I did, Terry was one of my headliners. What kind of animals do crap like this?"

"The two-legged kind that patronize shitholes like this," Muldoon tells him.

"You guys create your own problems the way you do things."

George just glared at him.

"I have nothing else to say to you, go fight crime."

George turned his back on them and watched a listless dancer hug a pole.

The detectives left. Morelli confronted Muldoon.

"Tone it down, big man, you get confrontational with guys like George, we will hear about it downtown."

"Yeah, perish the thought they don't get their end of it," Muldoon griped.

"Like you don't have your own little deals going on," Morelli snickered.

Muldoon just glared at him. "Let's hit 'the Deuce' one joint at a time," Morelli suggested.

Wayne and Howie were two gay hustlers. Wayne was a burly black-haired man with a pockmarked face. Howie was a slim guy with long blonde hair. They were known in the area as The Juiced Fruits. Never sober, considered harmless, they were anything but. Especially Wayne. A bad temper fueled by the drug of the day, PCP. Right now, they were very nervous.

"People are looking, people are talking, we fucked up real bad, Wayne."

"Bitch got in my face, I don't take shit from any fuckin cunt," Wayne snarled. "Besides, we got what we came for, now we just have to sit on it for a bit."

"For how long," asked Howie. "I want to get out of this town."

"When I get the word, we cut the pie," Wayne told him.

"It better be soon, everyone is looking for this." Howie nodded to the suitcase in the corner.

"No one is lookin' this way, we're covered, just keep to business as usual until we get the heads up."

Tondawanda Pete was the manager of Blackjack Books. Owned by mobster 'Bikini Joe', it was right in the middle of 42nd Street. Open 24/7 the place had been busted for prostitution, obscenity, and other violations. The busts were a joke because within 24 hours of any bust, Blackjack Books would be open again. Pete was a Vietnam vet who had done two tours, one because he was drafted, the other for revenge. At 6 feet and 2 inches, he was 220 pounds of someone you didn't want to get sideways with.

Pete always wore a bandana and was usually unshaven. His 2nd in command was Leon, a career 'bouncer' for bookstores and massage parlors. Leon was a stocky, muscular Cuban from Miami. The murders were a big topic of conversation.

"This is some fucked up shit, Leon, the boys are really pissed," Pete explained.

"Yeah, I hear they may put up some money to find out who did it," Leon replied.

"Had to be someone not from around here, no one in the know would try shit like this."

"Yeah, someone was watching where it was going. No one would try to take it from Eddie, that's a given."

"I don't trust that cunt, Shelly, but Marty does for some reason."

"Yeah, that I don't get, she keeps trying to open more theaters. She's competition that we don't need."

Just then the door opened, and the two guys weren't customers. "Oh shit, Car 54 where are you just arrived," muttered Pete.

Morelli and Muldoon walked in.

"What can we do for New York's finest today?"

"You can stick your attitude up your ass and start talking," Muldoon snarled.

"About what? The weather? Been nice the last few days, cool breeze from the..."

"Shut the fuck up, you know what we mean, who killed those girls?"

"If I knew that, you'd be the last person I'd tell, there is a reward out ya know."

"So, you know something."

"No, I don't know shit, no one does, if they did, they'd take care of it."

"You're an asshole, Pete, fuckin low life, bet you think you're tough".

"Throw your badge and gun on the counter, then I'll show you who's tough."

"Yeah, big bad Nam vet, you can kiss my ass."

"I'll say it again, put your shit on the counter and let's go. Got a problem with that, Morelli? You going to jump in?"

"Brian," Morelli said, "We don't need this."

"Fuck you, and fuck him, I'm going to kick his ass."

Muldoon put his gun and badge on the counter.

"Leon, keep Sal honest," Pete said.

Pete swung open the door to his counter, hitting Muldoon across the knees, Muldoon dropped the leather sap he had hidden.

"I knew you would try that shit, you mick bastard," Pete snarled.

Pete uncorked a vicious punch to Muldoon's nose. Blood and snot flew out of it. Pete kicked the bigger man in the shin. Muldoon bent down and caught a big uppercut that staggered him. Pete bored in, but

Muldoon swung a backhand that connected. Pete shook that off and spit blood in Muldoon's face. Muldoon threw a punch at Pete's head, but it caught him in the shoulder and spun him to the floor. Muldoon went to kick him, but Pete grabbed his foot and shoved. Muldoon fell backwards into a rack of books. Pete jumped on him and started beating a tattoo on his face and shoulders.

Cold steel was on Pete's neck as Morelli pulled his gun on him. Leon had a ball bat and was going to take Morelli's head off. "Everybody freeze," Morelli yelled. "I fuckin' said freeze, what the fuck is wrong with you assholes, I'll shoot you if you don't get off him." Pete, hands in the air, got off of Muldoon. Morelli, gun still out, used one arm to help Muldoon up. Muldoon was a mess, face bloody, clothes ripped and really pissed off.

"It's over," Morelli told them. "Now I have to go arrest some nigger to cover this up."

Muldoon glared hate out of swollen eyes.

"It's not fuckin done, you scumbag, you got payback comin'."

"Good, next time leave your toys home, tough guy"

"Brian, let's get you to Saint Vincent's and..."

"Fuck you all, I'll go myself."

Muldoon staggered out to the street.

"Pete, he's not going to forget this," Morelli told him.

"Fuck him," Pete snarled. "I respect you, Sal, but your partner can go fuck himself."

"Just watch your ass, and let me know if you hear anything"

Pete just waved him off. Morelli went looking for Muldoon.

Leon watched Morelli leave, then went to put together the racks that got knocked down during the fight.

"You ok, Pete?"

"Better than he is about now. I knew he'd pull that crap."

"Should we be worried?"

"Not we, just me, he ain't going to forget that. If Morelli didn't bust it up, he wasn't going to quit. I'd have to knock him out or kill his ass. He's too stupid to know he's beat, he can't accept that, he would have kept coming until I put him down. Just do me a favor, if I ever get jackpotted, get me out. That bastard gets me in a cell, I'm a dead man."

"You got it, boss."

"That hippie prick is a dead man," Muldoon snarled.

He and Morelli just rousted a black PCP dealer. They claimed he attacked Muldoon.

"I just covered your ass on this one, Brian, stop fucking with these guys."

"Fuckin wops don't scare me, I got the..."

"Shut up, I'm sick of dealing with this shit from you, I'm a goddamn wop, you need another partner? Fine, I'll put in a request."

"Sal, you know I..."

"I don't know what your problem is, but they run this shithole, we don't. We get taken care of. Pete runs his mouth to certain people, you may be giving out parking tickets in Harlem, ok?"

Muldoon wanted to say something, but he couldn't. Getting transferred would not only be demeaning, but it would also mean loss of revenue.

"So now what," asked Muldoon.

"We keep looking, someone had to hear something."

Wayne and Howie were at Stonewall. Wayne was trying to sell some PCP he just scored. When it became obvious to the bartender what he was doing, he was told to drink up and leave.

"Why don't you make me leave, you big pussy," Wayne responded. The bartender just smiled, then waved over two large men who were bouncers.

"Escort these gentleman out," he told them. Wayne was messed up, but not stupid enough to try these guys. The two sulked out.

"Let's try Topps, we should be able to unload some of this there,"

Wayne suggested. Topp's was a real bad bar located on the right-hand side of the Deuce, close to 7th Avenue. It was in the area considered no man's land, two grindhouses, The New Amsterdam and the Harris, and a gay bath house, the New Barracks, were in close proximity.

Back at Blackjack Books, things had calmed down. The usual array of human flotsam was wandering in and out. The girls were busy in the live peeps. Blackjack had an open window policy, no glass between the patrons and the performers. Girls peddled sex to the adventurous perverts who didn't mind sucking a spit slobbered boob or getting a quick blow job. Busts were common at Blackjack's. Not that it mattered, palms were greased, and the problems vanished.

"Leon, watch the front," Pete ordered. "I'm going to grab a couple of slices, you want anything?"

"No, boss, I'm good, bon appetite."

Pete went to a pizza joint close by. He knew by beating up Muldoon, he was going to have problems down the road.

"Maybe I should just move on," he thought. Then he laughed to himself, "Unfit for conventional employment," he chuckled.

He sat at the counter and ordered two slices. He watched the parade of street walkers, cruisers, and tourists go in and out.

"Fun fuckin city," he muttered. "Time to go back to work."

He returned to find Leon agitated.

"Lily just went into your office," Leon told him, "And that creepy Darby just followed her in."

Pete said nothing, he went to his office and kicked the door open. A skinny guy with his pants down was on top of a blonde woman.

"Get the fuck off of my cot," he screamed. He grabbed the guy by his collar and flung him across the room.

"You," he yelled at the girl, who was making no move to cover up. "I fuckin told you no tricks in my office, you're out of here."

Darby was then stupid enough to open his mouth.

"It ain't what you think, she tripped, and I was helping her get up."

"And in doing so, your pants came down and you fell right into her pussy. You're going to give me $50 right now or I'm going beat the shit out of you."

"$50 for what, she just ..."

"She just got herself fired and you're buying me a new cot because I'll be fucked if I'm going to sleep with your cooties. Give it up, now." Darby started pulling 20 dollar bills out of his pocket. Pete grabbed 3 of them.

"Where's my fuckin change," Darby asked.

"Sin tax, now get the fuck out of here."

Darby scurried out the door.

Pete turned to Lily

"In case you're deaf, you're officially fired."

"You can't fire me, only Joe can."

"Wanna bet? Go cry to him, go cry to Marty, hey, even go cry to DB. I run this place and you're gone."

"You'll be sorry, you can't..."

"Honey, I just did, there's the door."

Throwing threats over her shoulder, Lily stormed out.

"I'm going to have to burn that cot," Pete told Leon.

"Sorry boss, we got busy, and I didn't see her, I saw her let that creepy Darby in, then she locked the door."

"It's not your fault, I knew she would pull this shit. Fuck her, she's gone, and sucking Joe's dick isn't getting her back in here."

At Topps, things weren't exactly working out for Wayne and Howie. After trying to make a sale, Wayne was pit bulled by a huge black man and told that was 'his territory' and leave before you get hurt. Howie got Wayne out the door before the blades came out. Wayne was full of PCP and alcohol, not a good combination. Before Howie could stop him, Wayne went into Blackjack Books.

Wayne was less than subtle, he started approaching customers aggressively. "This is real good shit," he told them. Pete saw what was going on.

"Hey fruit loop, take you and that shit outside."

"What did you call me?" the PCP just shifted gears; Wayne reached into his pocket.

"I told you to get the fuck..."

Wayne ran to the counter and grabbed Pete by his collar. His straight razor was against Pete's neck. Blood started flowing. "I'll do you like I did those cunts..."

The front of the counter exploded. Pete kept a snub nose .38 under it and had just pulled the trigger. Wayne staggered back, blood pouring from a bullet wound in his chest. He looked shocked, but then came at Pete again. Blood running down his shirt, Pete fired two more shots, one missed, the other went through Wayne's left eye and out the back of his head. Wayne hit the floor; Howie ran for his life. Leon tried to stop the bleeding from Pete's slashed neck.

"Man, the cops will be here in a minute," Leon said.

"Fuck me, this piece isn't legal, I'm fucked, after that fight, I'm fucked if I go to the tombs."

The police came, guns drawn. Pete was going into shock. Leon tried to explain it as a robbery gone bad. The .38 was bagged. Paramedics arrived and were working on Pete's neck wound. Pete was read his rights. Reality hit Pete.

"Leon, call fuckin Joe, call Marty, hell, even call DB, I know who did it."

"Did what," a cop asked.

"Fuck you, Leon, tell them to make this go away, I fuckin know now, goddammit."

Howie ran to the first working pay phone he could find. He dialed a number and waited. Someone picked up.

"It's me, I gotta drop that thing off to you."

"It's too soon."

"It may be too late, Wayne is dead, he got stupid, before he died, he ran his mouth."

"You guys really fucked up."

"Worse than you could imagine. The guy is on his way to the Tombs. Wayne cut him, before the cops came, he told the other guy to call everyone who could get him out. He yelled he knew who did it."

"Ok, bring it over, but you don't get yours until things cool off."

"Fine, I'm on my way."

Howie delivered the suitcase. He figured it was time to get out of town. He went back to his place to get his stuff and found he had visitors.

Two men were waiting in his apartment.

"We can do this the easy way. Or we can beat it out of you, your choice, where is it?"

Howie told them where he took the suitcase. Howie was shot in the head.

One of the men made a call.

"Boss, you're not going to believe who is behind this."

"Ok, thrill me."

"Shelly, he told us Shelly set the whole thing up."

"Think he was lying?"

"No, he was scared shitless and thought he could walk."

"I have my doubts, she was never a problem, a pain in the ass, but never a real problem."

"So, what should we do?"

"Pay her a courtesy call, like you're just making sure she is all right. See how she reacts."

"And if she was behind it?"

"Put her out of business." The man hung up.

"We have business at the Venus," he told his partner. Shelly lived in an apartment over The Venus.

Shelly buzzed the two men in. The Venus was running its usual triple feature of porn.

"So how are you holding up, Shelly," one of the men asked.

"I'm still shook up, those poor girls, any idea who did it?"

"Well, we know who did it, because one of them tried some crazy shit at Blackjack's that got him dead. Strangely we had a chat with the other guy but didn't find the money."

"So they must have spent it on dope, which figures."

"No, Shelly, Howie told us that you have it."

"You believe some junkie fuck? This is bullshit, Joe, Marty, any of those guys will vouch for me. You come in here and accuse me of ripping off..."

"It's under her bed," a voice told them.

The men turned and saw that Beth came into the room.

"Her guy dropped it off, she set the whole thing up, her guy did this to me and she let him." Beth pulled the bandage off her face.

"Think I was going to forget this, you fuckin bitch? You let him cut me, then told me to live with it, fuck you."

Shelly went to say something but was backhanded. Duct tape went over her mouth and her hands were tied behind her.

"Miss Shelly has an appointment," one of the men told Beth. "I think you just got a better job, if you want it."

"I'll take it and you won't regret it," Beth said.

"Good, I'll tell your new boss and you can work the details out with him."

No one ever saw Shelly again, and things went back to normal. Or what passed for normal on 'the Deuce'.

• • • •

There was never an actual robbery. This story is based on some real events that I turned into a fictional tale. The language used is what you would have heard if you lived in that time period.

Blackjack Books was a real porn store in the middle of 42nd street. Robert 'DIB' Debernardo ran all the porn in NYC. He was also killed in an unsanctioned hit as he was owed 25K and rather than pay the debt, he was killed.

Topps Bar was at the end of The Deuce near 7th Avenue. Not a place you'd want to linger at.

Stonewall was the flash point for gay rights as because of police harassing the patrons, there was a full-scale riot. This shined a light on the gay community and the harassment they were dealing with.

Big George did really own the Merry Go Round and The Metropole. They were featured in the film Fear City, I left out his last name because I think I still owe him money.

The Doll was a theater that was part of the Avon Chain and Phil Prince and his wife performed there.

Eddie worked for Martin Hodas and collected all the quarters from the peep shows. He would cash then in a Chemical Bank, about 30K per week - 70's money.

Chelly Wilson owned The Venus and a couple of other theaters. Contrary to other things written about her, she did not own anything related to Avon Films and was considered a pain in the ass as she tried, with no success to expand her holdings.

Morelli and Muldoon mirrored the cops on the take or cops doing shakedowns.

Tonawanda Pete could have been any of the Vietnam vets that returned from the war too damaged to function. These guys found work in the sex trade as live show performers, bookstore managers or security for massage parlors. They were paid cash and that cash supplemented their disability benefits.

Leon was a career 'security guard' for massage parlors and other venues that I got friendly with back in the day.

Phil Prince and his wife, Teresita, were live sex show performers. She was killed while visiting a dealer friend who incurred the wrath of another dealer. Hence the title, Wrong Place, Wrong Time.

THE FIXER

1

My name is Vince, Vince Toricelli and I fix problems. Well, I try anyway. The last problem I fixed got me sent upstate for five years. Rather than expose myself, that 'problem' included a beat cop and a detective that were already on the pad. I was asked to correct the situation. I did and got sent away on 'vacation'. When the law is involved, precautions must be taken.

I was up for parole three years in. I didn't want it. Not that I liked being in the Gray Bar Hotel, but I was taken care of. Parole would mean that I had to report to someone for the next two years. I had work waiting for me, not the kind of work a parole officer would approve of. So, I did the five. I was 22 when I went in. Now I'm 27. I was also related to the Big Guy, which helped.

When I got out, they threw a big party for me. I got a blowjob from a classy whore in the back room. Wise guys praised me for being stand up and keeping my mouth shut. I wanted to go back to work. I needed to talk to someone about work. Marty and George 'The Hump' took me aside.

"Vince, we really appreciate you, you're a stand-up guy, Marty told him

"Thanks," I said, "when can I start earning?"

"John wants to give you something low key for a bit. A couple of these cops still may have a hardon for you," Marty told him.

"Ok, I get that, so what's the job?"

"Collections, easy work unless someone gets stupid. You get the massage joints; I'll give you a list. Every night, you make the rounds, say after midnight. Let the operators know who you are and that you represent us," George told him. "You get $500 a week, plus open tabs at any of our places."

"That sounds good for a start, George, and I appreciate it," I told him.

"Vince, do it and see how it goes. If there's no heat from that other incident, you'll move up. I know you like more action, and this will ease you back in."

Marty chimed in, "You're gonna need a partner in this, someone to watch your back, I have a guy."

"No, Marty, thanks, but no thanks, I'd rather get someone I know," I told him.

"That's fine, Vince," George told him, "Your guy gets $200 a week. Get him on board because you start this Saturday, three days from now." Well, now I knew what I had to do. It was June 1976, the year of The Big Bicentennial Celebration. America was celebrating its 200th Birthday. There were tall ships in the harbor. Business will be booming all over Times Square. I needed to get my ducks in a row, so to speak.

Now I must find a guy that I can trust to back me up. I decided to go to McGirrs, the pool hall where guys hung out. I get there and see two knock around guys, Nails Morgan and Cueball Jones.

"Well look who's back," Jones exclaimed. "When did you get out?"

"A couple of days ago, how are you guys doing?"

"Not bad," said Nails, "actually we've been doing real good as of late."

"Either of you looking for work? I just got a gig from The Hump and I need someone to watch my back. It pays $200 a week, cash."

"Vince," Jones said, "you've been gone for a while, things changed for Nails and me. We made a little score and we sorta invested wisely, so we are pretty flush right now. Appreciate the offer, but it's not for us."

"Well, that's fuckin great. Seriously, I'm glad for you guys. But can I count on you if I get in a jackpot?"

"Sure, Vinnie, we're friends, if we can help you out, just ask," answered Jones. The men shook hands and Vince left.

I was glad those guys had something going. But that didn't solve my problem. Either of them would have worked as they were stand up guys and backed down to no one. I still need someone. I remember a guy, Claude Hutto. We did a few things before I went away. I just had to find him. With that thought, I go back to McGirr's. Nails and Jones were shooting a game. "Hey guys, either of you know Claude Hutto?"

"Yeah, we see him around every so often," Jones replied.

"Where does he hang out?"

"The Terminal Bar."

"Thanks boys."

The Terminal Bar was directly across the street from Port Authority, right next to The Terminal Hotel, home of the ugliest $5 whores in New York City. The place was a true dive and good for, shall I say, less than legal activities. Claude Hutto was a tall guy, receding black hair, with hawk like features. He was perched on a bar stool with a Budweiser in front of him. I took the stool next to him.

"Well, look who's back in town. How ya doing Vince?"

"A lot better out here," I told him.

"No shit, I heard you're working for The Hump."

"You heard right, you lookin' for something?"

"A nice bag of weed, I'd be looking for if there was any?"

"No marywanna around?"

"Vince, with this fuckin Bicentennial they are watching everything. Tons of people coming in from all over. If I'd had a pussy, I'd make a fortune."

The two laughed over that.

"Seriously, Claude, you looking for work? I got a gig, but I need another guy."

"What's the job," Claude asked.

"Collections, every night I have to make the rounds. I need someone to watch my back."

"What's it pay?"

"$200 a week."

"Does that include sampling the pussy?"

"Considering where we are going, would you want this kind of pussy?"

Vince showed Claude the list.

"Yeah, I see what you mean, Holiday Hostesses, The Dating Room. Her Place, The Silver Slipper, The Meeting Room, no, don't want any of that. Such classy places though."

"So, are you interested?"

"Yeah, I could use a diversion, when do we start?"

"Saturday night, meet me by Blue's kiosk on the corner of 42nd and 8th and we'll make the rounds."

"Cool, thanks buddy, and if you see and grass, grab it for me."

I had forgotten that Claude was a pot head. Not my thing, but I did notice that no one was selling nickel bags on 'The Deuce'. Usually there were about a dozen guys, now nothing. One thing this country can do is shut down the borders tighter than a clam's ass. I had looked over my list and figured that it would take most of the night to make the rounds. I was supposed to be given an envelope. I would write the places name on it. It was a set amount, and I was never to open them. They went to the Hump and if it was short, he'd take care of it. Or send me to take care of it.

Massage parlors started after I left. Marty had taken a couple of bookstores that weren't doing well and turned them into parlors. There was a $10 cover charge that allowed you to undress in front of the model of your choice. That was it, you had to tip the girl for a hand job or blowjob. Guys that came in expecting a real 'massage' got chased out. Because of the Bicentennial, business was really good.

• • • •

2

I MET CLAUDE AND OUR first stop is The Dating Room. The Dating Room was on 42nd Street on the 4th floor of what was a suite of offices. The place charged $13, ten for the visit, three for a 'membership'. You got a card that you would get punched for each visit. When you hit ten visits, you got a freebie. We take the elevator up to the 4th floor and walk into a disaster.

Leon, the door man is bleeding. The boss, Extra Large Marge is screaming at me. "I'm supposed to have protection, you wop fuck, you call this protection?" Marge was a veteran madam and weighed over 300 pounds. Right now, smoke was coming out of her ears. "What happened," I asked. Marge goes off. "We got robbed, that's what happened, three fuckin spics robbed us, I'm supposed to have protection, you gotta make this right, Vince."

"Ok, let me talk to Leon." I take Leon to a back room. "First, are you ok?"

"No, I'm fuckin hurtin' and I'm pissed."

"Weren't you working at Blackjack?"

"We got busted again, Pete's in jail, so they needed a guy here because the regular guy is sick."

"Ok, tell me what happened?"

"Three guys come up; I go to pat them down like I do everyone. I bend down and one hits me in the head, then they all start kicking me. One slaps a girl then they tell Marge to give them the money. Marge tells them to get the fuck out. They push her out of the way and clean out the drawer."

"Can you ID these pricks?"

"Yeah, I can."

"Let's go for a walk. Claude, stay here, we'll be back."

I take Leon and head up the block to Fascination, a pinball arcade.

"You think they are in here," Leon asks.

"It's a hangout for scumbags and they are scumbags."

We go inside to the crashing din of loud noise and flashing lights.

"There's the cocksucker." Leon points to a tall guy with a cut off Levi jacket and a beret.

"You sure?"

"Positive."

I hand him a sap. "Keep the other two off my back."

Now I walk up to the guy, grab the back of his head and smash his face though the glass. Blood spurts. One of his boys comes at me and Leon cracks the sap over the back of his head. Two down. I punch the third guy's teeth out. I go through the bloody guy's pocket and find the money and my envelope. I kick the shit out of the guy on the floor. "Rob my joint, you cocksucker". I feel ribs break. "Listen to me, all of you motherfuckers listen up, do not fuck with me or my places, I'll fuckin' kill the next little prick who tries something." I kick the guy in the head and walk out.

"Jesus Christ, you don't fuck around, do you," asked Leon.

"No, I don't, sorry you got jacked, but after that little show I doubt anyone will try that again. We'll go back and I'll give Marge the money and keep the envelope."

We go back to the Dating Room and find Claude in deep conversation with one of the massage girls. "Did you get the fuckin' money," Marge bellowed.

"Yeah here it is, I fixed the problem because that's what I do." I hand her the money.

"They won't be back, not unless they want to die."

"What did you do," Marge asked or snorted, she did snort a lot.

"He fucked them up," Leon added, "and fucked them up big time."

"I'm done here, Claude, let's get back to work."

So Claude and I go to our next stop, Holiday Hostesses right up the street from Blackjack Books. The place had about three girls of questionable health, sitting around in worn out lingerie. A guy called Bobo was in charge. Bobo was big and sweaty. He wore a t-shirt even in the winter.

He had what I thought was a brick on the counter.

"Doing a little side masonry work, Bobo?"

"It ain't a brick, it's a fruit cake."

"Looks a little stale."

"Listen, there hasn't been a fruit cake made here since 1948."

"Well, that's interesting." Claude rolls his eyes, so I know he must know where this is going.

"Vince, if someone gave you a fuckin fruit cake, would you eat it?"

"No."

"Do you actually know anyone who has eaten one, and I'm not talking the ones Grandma makes all loaded with rum and shit, I'm talking these industrial ones."

"No, can't say that I have."

"So, people return them because it's a shitty gift. They get sent to this big warehouse in Wisconsin or someplace and they repackage them and ship them back out next Christmas. Then when they get like this," Bobo thumps the cake on the counter for effect, "They use them to build containers to store nuclear waste in."

"Damn, Bobo, you know, I never knew that. Thanks for that bit of pertinent information."

Bobo had a big smile. "You're welcome."

"C'mon, Claude, let's go." We leave and I turn to Claude. "You fuck, you knew he was going to do that."

"Never ask Bobo anything unless you want to spend time hearing shit like you just heard."

"You think it's funny?"

"Yeah, I do, the look on your face when he got going was priceless."

"Good, from now on you go in, I'll wait downstairs."

Next stop was the Lucky Lady on 46th Street. This was a street level parlor.

"This used to be Chiba Street," Claude told Vince.

"What the hell is Chiba?"

"There was this movie, The Street Fighter, Kung Fu film, big hit. The star was Sonny Chiba. These weed dealers got some real potent shit and called it Chiba. Damn, Vince, every weekend there was a parade of cars from Jersey jamming up this street trying to score some Chiba. What I wouldn't give for a joint of that now."

"When did that movie come out?"

"A couple of years ago."

"Guess I missed it."

"It was pretty cool, actually, here's the place, but I remember it as Her Place."

"George clued me that this was a trouble spot. It's been busted twice already and that drag bar doesn't help." Vince pointed across the street to Sally's Hideaway. A black drag queen was mincing around outside.

"These heshes turn tricks out here in cars and that alley. The cops come, bust them and that scares off customers."

"Not our problem, let's go in," Claude said.

The Lucky Lady was decked out on Leopard print. A guy was running toward the door with a horrified look on his face. A half-naked brunette was chasing him screaming. "I don't care how much you want to tip me, you smelly bastard, you can't come in ten minutes, you're gone." She looks at me.

"You got a problem?" No but after being locked up for 5 years, she definitely had my attention. She was tall, about 5'7", waist length brown hair and piercing green eyes.

"No, but I like the way you handled yourself."

"Bad enough I have to suck cock to pay my rent, but at least the motherfuckers could bathe."

"What's your name? I'm Vince."

"Well, hi Vince, I'm Connie, some people here call me Connie the Cunt." She glared at the manager. The manager was Spiro, a guy with a pompadour and thin mustache. He hands me the envelope.

"You want something better?"

"Like what, and Vince, this isn't getting you into my pants if that's the offer."

"Lady, you have huge balls, you're Italian, right?"

"I am, so what? You heard Spiro, I'm just a whore."

"So, I try to take care of my people, and you're a whore by choice, want to change that?"

"How?"

"I make a call, to a place where you won't be disrespected."

"What kind of place?"

"An uptown penthouse with showers for the clients, clean rooms and better money. Yeah, you're still screwing for a living, but it's up to you."

"What's in it for you?"

"I'm establishing myself; I was gone for a bit. Now I'm back. Honestly, I like that you're a tough broad, you don't back down. Maybe I can use you for something else down the road, but for now, that's what I can offer. You want me to make the call?"

"Yes, thank you, sorry if I was a cunt to you, I'm just so tired of getting fucked over."

I called The Retreat on East 43rd Street. I spoke to a guy named Bruno. "Bruno, I'm sending a lady down to see you, I think she'll be an asset to your place."

"Sure, Vince, what's her name?"

"She goes by Connie; she's a class act and I'd consider it a personal favor."

"Not a problem, Vince, good to have you back."

"Thanks, Bruno, I'll tell her to drop by tomorrow."

Vince and Claude left to their next spot, Cupid's Retreat on 42nd Street. After picking up the envelope, Claude muttered, "I have seen some really weird shit, but that place just took first prize."

"You mean the tents," Vince chuckled.

TWO FISTED TALES OF TIMES SQUARE

"Connie a problem," I ask.

"After tonight she won't be, I'm firing her ass."

"Guess she is a problem."

"She thinks who she is, she's a whore, don't care how goo[d she] looks, she's a whore doing a whore's work. She can go down t[he] avenue and work there. She's done here."

"I need to use your office."

"You want a blowjob, use her room."

"Spiro, you're not listening, I just asked you something, and [you] just gave me shit. Do you need a reminder about who you work for[?]"

"Sure, tough guy, you want a piece of ass? Go for it."

"This has nothing to do with me wanting a piece of ass but [has] everything to do with your fuckin attitude."

"Fuck, you, go talk to the whore."

"Connie, I need a word with you." I lead her to Spiro's office in th[e] back.

"I don't blow managers for favors," she tells me.

"I'm not looking for that, I fix things, you have a problem that needs fixing."

"I don't have any problems."

"Yeah, you do, like you're outta work after I leave here."

"What did that greasy little prick tell you?"

"That you act like your shit don't stink, and my observation is that you don't belong here."

"You don't think I belong here."

"Yeah, because look at you, then look at your coworkers. What got you into this anyway?"

"A sick mother and a no-good husband. When I decided to help my mom, he walked, just left one night and never came back. I answered an ad in The Village Voice. That was three months ago. I hate this place and I hate that jerk off," She motions toward Spiro.

"He's a snake."

"Yeah, c'mon, who would have taken a loft, put up six army surplus pup tents, and charge guys to screw hookers in them?"

"It's genius, Claude, pure genius, and perfect for the Times Square outdoorsman."

"Well, it beats out that topless shoeshine joint, all the comfort of a pay toilet. What's the next stop?"

"200 east 14th Street, lets hop the subway."

200 East 14th Street was on the 2nd floor and had no real name. The girls were not attractive, but friendly, and the manager, Perry, was very polite.

"Not much going on here," remarked Claude.

"This place has been here before I went away. Very low keyed, they have their regulars and never have any problems."

They finished up the smaller place and Claude asked if they were going to the east side to The Retreat, the Harem, the upscale places.

"No," said Vince, "I guess someone else does that, I'm just going by the list. But it's 3AM, were done, let's go for a nightcap."

"Sounds good, I like this deal, work 3 hours, not bad at all."

"And only one incident, let's go to 44, I got the first round."

Bars closed in New York City at 4am, for professional drinkers, other places opened at 4am. Things were good, Vince thought. Too bad things didn't stay that way.

• • • •

3

PACO MORALES WAS BITTER, but ambitious. He had been doing seven years upstate. That brought him into contact with Vince. He envied Vince, Vince took no shit and had protection. Paco had protection too as he joined a gang, The Latino Kings. First, he was their errand boy, then as a full-fledged member, he joined in the spoils. He like raping the new prisoners, he was at heart, a fuckin punk, he needed protection as he was only 5'6" and weighed 120 pounds.

He noticed the wops didn't bother with what he considered 'fun'. Paco started getting a bad attitude toward those guys. He ran his mouth to his 'crew' about how they should be taken down. Paco kept saying that they should take out Vince. The truth was that the gang wanted nothing to do with the wops, but Paco was obsessed. When he had a plan to get Vince in the showers, they said they'd back him. They didn't. Paco had a sharpened toothbrush handle. Vince was toweling off when Paco drifted in. Vince wasn't stupid and word had gotten back about Paco.

Vince acted like nothing was wrong, but he was ready. When Paco got a little too close, Vince decked him with a quick right hand. Paco's 'shiv' hit the floor. Vince picked it up, grabbed Paco's face and gashed his cheek twice. "Next time I'll gut your greasy ass." Vince threw the shiv in his face and left Paco bleeding.

Paco didn't shut up and told anyone who would listen that Vince was dead. His days were numbered. What Paco didn't know was that his 'crew' were told that if they backed this idiot, there would be dire repercussions. They knew better than to mess with the Italians. Paco was ignored, which further fueled his rage. Paco became a 'model' prisoner. Paco had heard that Vince would have a sweet set up when he got out and he now wanted what Vince had. Vince had put Paco in the back of his mind. After all, he was in for seven years and still had three to go.

Fate is a tricky bitch. Paco made parole. He saw his parole officer every week and behaved. But he was enquiring about Vince and what he was doing. Soon he had it all figured out. He would kill Vince, then claim his territory. But Paco didn't understand the complexities of the area. Say something stupid, threaten someone connected, or try to get in on someone else's hustle, word will get back to people. Stupidity had its price. And Paco was stupid.

Paco was in Club 45 nursing a beer. The bartender was a guy in his 50's named Charley. Charley was about 5' 9" with a craggy face and thick salt and pepper hair. Right now, he was listening to this punk run his mouth. "You know a guy named Vince, he's a dago that works around here," Paco asked Charley. The 'dago' crack didn't go well with Charley as his last name was D'Amato.

"Can't say that I do," Charley replied. "Get a lot of people through here."

Paco snorted. "I heard he knows everyone, made man and all that. I was in stir with him, he's a punk and I'm going to take his ass out."

Charley frowned at this, he knew Vince and Vince was no punk. "So, you're going to kill this guy Vince, why?"

"For this," Paco pointed to the scars on his cheek.

"Well, good luck with that."

"I don't need luck, he does. I gotta take a piss."

Paco went to the rest room.

Charley made a quick call to The Hump. "George, it's Charley over at 45. Listen, there's a spic in here that Vince must have fucked up when he was away. He's talking about killing Vince, you should warn him."

"Let me find Vince," George said. "See if you can keep that guy there, I'll send Vince over."

"I'll buy him a round and keep him talking."

"Thanks, Charley, I owe you one."

George started calling around for Vince. He finally found him in McGirr's.

"Pop, it's George, is Vince hanging around?"

"Yeah, let me get him, Vince, ya got a call." Vince took the phone.

"Vince, it's George, did you have a problem with some jerk off when you were in?"

"Yeah, some Puerto Rican tried to make a name for himself. I fucked him up. He won't be out for another couple of years. Why?"

"Got a news flash for you, he musta made parole because right now he's at Club 45 bending Charley's ear about how he's gonna kill you and take your spot."

"Oh, really? Time to put that little cocksucker back in his sandbox."

"Vince, don't do anything crazy, you don't want to go back, just fix it, ok?"

"Sure George, I'll fix it right now." Vince hung up and looked for someone. Nails Morgan was finishing a game of 8 ball.

"Nails, you want to make a quick C-note?"

"Why sure."

"Then let's take walk."

"To where?"

"Club 45, Charley needs something fixed."

Vince and Nails practically marched to Club 45.

"Charley", Vince yelled, "You better call the cops about that broken window." Paco looked up from his drink and saw Vince. He went for something in his pocket, but it was too late.

"Nails, throw this cocksucker though the window." Nails grabbed Paco and a switchblade fell out of his hand. One hand on the belt another hand around the neck and Paco flew through the window in a shower of glass and bounced off a parked car.

Vince slipped Nails a folded bill. "Take off, Bro, I'm good now." Nails nodded and left.

Vince took a bottle of something and went outside. He picked up Paco and forced the booze down his throat. "I told you, motherfucker, I warned you and now you're going back." Vince beat the shit out of him, then put the knife back in his pocket. "I count three parole violations, buddy, have fun for a few years and if I ever see you again, I'll fuckin kill you."

Vince left before the cops came. When the cops came, Charley told them that this guy got crazy after drinking and jumped through the window. One cop just rolled his eyes as he cuffed Paco. Hit with like three parole violation, Paco was finished. His big mouth got him in the jackpot. Vince was praised for the way he handled the situation.

A month went by, and Vince and Claude settled into a comfortable groove. It wouldn't remain comfortable.

• • • •
4

VINCE WAS AT GEORGE 'The Hump's' dropping off the envelopes when Cueball Jones came in and whispered something to George.

"Really? Why didn't Pop call?"

"Because this crazy motherfucker ripped the phone off the wall," Jones told him.

"Vince," George ordered, "take Claude and fix this mess."

Vince motioned to Jones. "What's going on?"

"This big, hairy fucker comes in, plays a game of pool and loses. Then he refused to pay off and beat the shit out of the guy. Pop goes to call you or the cops, then he rips the phone off the wall. Then he tells everyone that this is 'their' place from now on and he gets $100 a day for protecting it," Jones finished.

"Any idea who he is?"

"No, but he's wearing colors, The Hell's Angels."

"What the fuck is this shit? We never had a problem with them, they pretty much stay on the Lower East side. This clown have a name?"

"I think it's Dennis."

"Ok, I need to talk to someone." Vince went to a pay phone and called around until he got the number he was looking for. He called the number.

"I need to talk to Sandy," Vince said. Someone put Sandy on the phone.

"Sandy, this is Vince Toricelli, you guys looking to expand or something?"

"No, what the fuck are you talking about?"

"Some motherfucker, wearing your club colors, just fucked up McGirrs and says that's it's your place now and has to pay for protection."

"That's bullshit, Vince, I don't know anything about this, the guy have a name?"

"Dennis".

"That cocksucker? He got tossed out of the Los Angeles club, he should have turned in his colors. Now he's here, saying he represents us? Fuck that noise, we'll come and collect him."

"Let me pack him up for you, he did some damage and I want to send a message."

"Good, call me at this number when he's ready," Sandy finished.

"Claude, go buy me a bottle of Visine Eye Drops," Vince ordered.

"Eyes bothering you, Vince?"

"Just go get it and meet me at McGirrs."

Vince and Cueball went to the pool hall. The big biker, Dennis was at the bar downing beer after beer. Vince ignored him. He motioned Pops to the side. "Give me a roll of that plastic you use to wrap sandwiches with," Vince ordered. Vince took the roll and went into the Men's Room. He wrapped plastic over the top of the bowl and lowered the seat on it. Then he hung an out of order sign on the door.

Claude arrived and handed Vince the Visine. Vince went behind the bar.

"Hey asshole," Dennis yelled to him, "give me a fuckin beer."

Vince studied the man; he was about 6'3" and about 300lbs. You just made this really easy Vince thought. Vince spiked the beer with a few drops of Visine. Dennis downed the beer and belched.

Vince walked over to Claude. "He's going to be in a world of shit in about ten minutes," Vince told him.

Word spread though McGirrs that something was about to happen. They all watched the big biker. Suddenly, Dennis turned pale. He grabbed his gut, then headed toward the Men's Room.

"Hey, it's out of order," Vince told him.

"Then you can clean it after I'm done," Dennis sneered.

Dennis went in, and Vince padlocked the door. He went out to a pay phone and called Sandy. "Come and pick up your garbage, but you better bring a tarp and gloves."

"What kind of shit am I dealing with here?"

"You just answered your own question." Vince hung up.

Dennis squatted on the bowl as his bowels let loose. Shit flew everywhere, even in his face. He couldn't control his bowels and kept on shitting. The crowd was laughing at the noise coming from the can. But then the stench crept out. Dennis was pounding at the door, but no one was going to open it. Sandy and his guys arrived.

"He's in the can," Vince said, "something he ate, I think." Vince took off the padlock. Dennis staggered out, his pants down around his ankles, and he was covered with his own shit.

"Jesus Christ, Vince, remind me never to piss you off. Ace, get that tarp out of the van, I'm not getting poop on it." They draped a tarp over Dennis and hustled him out. Vince didn't want to know his fate.

"Sorry about the crapper, Pop."

"You're not gonna clean it?"

"Fuck no." Vince peeled off a $50 bill. "Hire someone."

Vince and Claude went back to see George. "Did you straighten things out," he asked.

"Yeah, they'll be no more problems with him or that club."

"Vince, you've done good for, me, you too, Claude, so I'm doubling your pay and you guys take care of things that need to be taken care of."

"Thanks, George, we appreciate this, we will be your eyes and ears and things will be taken care of." Vince and Claude left.

"Wow, we must have really impressed him," Claude said.

"We did, they appreciate loyalty. I fixed things five years ago, now I'm fixing things again. Let go get a drink or two."

• • • •

During the summer of '76 security was so tight that you couldn't find any weed on the east coast.

Gee, what happened?

The Visine trick was used by bartenders on rowdy patrons. It gave people the uncontrollable shits.

Marty was Martin Hodas, Papa of the Peeps.

Sandy was Sandy Alexander, former president of the New York Hell's Angels Chapter.

THE ACQUISITION

It was in Romania in the early 80's, an American brothel owner, Omar, has come to purchase a specific woman. The directions led to a rundown warehouse. His contact was a man named Hiram.

"Do you have the merchandise we agreed on," Omar asked.

"If you have the 100K American dollars," Hiram answered.

"No," Omar replied waving an attaché case.

"I have my dirty shorts; do you have a laundry service?"

"Of course, I have it, do you think I came all this way to stiff you?"

"You joke, of course," Hiram said. "I know you are a man of your word."

"Well, let see if you are, I need to see the merchandise."

Hiram opens the door to let Omar and his assistant, Clyde into the musty smelling building. Pushing aside the cobwebs, Hiram opens a locked door. Inside is a naked woman strapped to a gurney. Her flesh is alabaster pale and her red hair fans out behind her head.

"Very pretty," remarks Omar, "And," glancing at her crotch, "a natural redhead."

"So, my friend, you are satisfied with the merchandise?" Omar hands Hiram the case. "Feel free to count it."

"No need, we are both honorable men." Hiram takes the case.

Omar turns to Clyde. "Go in and pack her up the way I told you, and don't fuck around, she's deadly."

"You got it, Boss." Clyde goes into the room.

"I have to get this package to the docks before dawn," Omar explains to Hiram. "The captain will look the other way; you do have those export documents in order?"

"Yes, everything was done the way you requested. It took some..." a horrific scream stopped the conversation. Clyde staggers out of the room, blood pouring from a gash in his neck. Omar was livid.

"I told you not to mess with her, you stupid fuck."

Clyde moaned, "I just wanted to.."

"Sample my merchandise? I hope it was worth your life."

"Boss, you can't.."

"You're a loose end and I can't have that." Omar shakes his arm and a .38 derringer slides into his hand. He shoots Clyde in the head.

"You have to kill the brain, then the body dies," Omar uttered in disgust.

Hiram had locked the door. The woman was pounding on it.

"Clyde freed her, you can't do anything until dawn, she's too dangerous after tasting blood."

"Well, there is one thing I can do."

"What would that be?"

"Tie up another loose end." Omar shoots Hiram in the head.

Omar went to his vehicle and used a car phone.

"I need a cleanup right now and something picked up and taken to the docks after dawn, got it?" Omar hung up and looked at the room.

"Money is money, but free is better. This little vampire is going to make me rich."

Omar was a tall, bald man with a goatee and piercing eyes. Originally from Algeria, he left that part of the world when one of his 'deals' went sideways. He wound up in NYC in the early 70's. He found his niche in the sex trade. A string of street level brothels and massage parlors got him seed money. Of course, the local Mafioso had to wet their beaks. If he paid them tribute, he was allowed to operate and grow.

Omar had a plan, he wanted to open an upscale joint for high rollers with, shall we say, different tastes. As his bankroll increased, he looked for a piece of property he could grab cheap. A biker bar, The Anchor, was on East 4th Street. Its main patrons were the NYC Chapter of the Hell's Angels. The building had four apartments over the bar, perfect for Omar's plan. What he didn't need was a problem with the bikers.

Ever the politician and possessing a huge pair of balls, Omar visited the biker's clubhouse and laid out his plans. "You gentlemen are not good for the business that I intend to run, so I'll make you this offer. I'll make a monthly contribution to your club and hire four of your guys to be security for my place. There are plenty of other bars close by, Otto's Shrunken Head, the Double Down, the Continental, take your pick."

The chapter president, Sandy, spoke up. "We need a minute," he motioned his sergeant at arms into a side room. "This guy has a big pair, I'll give him that, the bread he is offering will pay our monthly expenses. Plus, he's mobbed up, he has to be to operate like this. I say we go for it, this bar sucks anyway, at least Otto's has bands on weekends."

Gonzo, the sergeant at arms said, "So all we are giving up is a shot and a beer joint, we get our rent paid, I don't see a downside."

"Neither do I," replied Sandy. "You want the bouncer job?"

"Sure, sounds like something right up my alley." Gonzo was five feet nothing and had a beard that hung down to his belt buckle.

"Ok," said Sandy, "lets seal the deal."

Omar waited patiently. The group came out of the room.

"We have a deal," Sandy told him. The two men shook on it.

"My associate, Gonzo, would make a great head of security," Sandy told Omar in a voice that was non-negotiable.

"Pleased to have you on board," Omar told him. "Let me explain to you how I want this done". The two men went outside to talk.

"You do realize that I'll be running an upscale place here," Omar explained.

"So I need even tempered people here, not hot heads. We want people to feel safe and spend money, so your crew must be nice, unless I tell them to not be nice, understood?"

"There won't be any problems," Gonzo assured him. "I have a couple of guys that are tough, but laid back."

"Fine," said Omar. "I'll be closing the place for a month or so to get it renovated."

Omar had seed money, 100K. The local mob had offered to back him for a huge chunk of the place, but Omar politely turned them down. Partners he didn't need. He had the place gutted, except for the mahogany bar. That he had refurbished. He turned each of the apartments into 'playrooms', but kept one apartment for his main attraction, Lilith, as he decided to name her. His business model was that anything sexual could be had for a price.

He would hire top tier sex workers. Dominatrices, transsexuals, party boys, a tattooed girl, and the ultimate fuck. He had stored his prize in a warehouse. The box was wrapped in garlic and had a large crucifix on top of it. Inside the box, she seethed in anger. She needed to feed; her strength was low from being in this prison. But most of all, she wanted revenge.

While construction was going on, Omar decided to advertise his place. He kept The Anchor name. He had business cards printed up that said, 'A Safe Harbor to Drop Your Anchor'. He stopped by the office of Screw Magazine to place a full-page ad. He explained to the editor, Eric, that The Anchor would have something for everyone, including the Ultimate Fuck.

"What the hell is the Ultimate Fuck," Eric asked.

"You know how hot a pussy can get, how good that feels? Well, this is just the opposite, a pussy so cold that it sears your soul, it takes you to a place you have never been before. Did you ever screw a vampire? I mean a real vampire."

Eric laughed, "Can't say that I have."

"I'm going to let you have one on me, that way you can tell your readers what The Anchor has for them. I'll be back in touch when we have our 'sample the wares party.'"

Omar's next stop was the notorious Blackjack Books in the middle of 42nd Street. Omar approached the night manager, a surly bastard called Tondawanda Pete. A grizzled veteran of that street, he eyed Omar with suspicion. Omar was too well dressed for this place. Omar

gave Pete his card, then gave him his spiel. Omar was so animated in his description
that Pete's hand closed over the long piece of heater hose packed with ball bearings that he kept under the counter.

"I should knock this asshole out on general principles," Pete thought.

When Omar was through, Pete glared at him.

"Obviously you're connected to someone, so I'll just warn you that if I give this card to my boss, you'll have another partner, and that partner will own your ass." Pete warned him.

"Nice that the HA may have your back, but we both know who runs this city."

Pete flipped the card back to Omar. "Get lost," Pete told him.

Omar was pissed at Pete's reaction, but a second look told him Pete was no joke. A beard covered the scarred face, his arms were tattooed, and Omar spotted a Marine Corps insignia. Pete gave Omar the stare. Omar left. Leon, the store's security, stepped out for a smoke. "Hey mister," he said to Omar, "try peddling that in places like the Hellfire Club and The Vault."

"Where are these places," Omar asked.

"Give me 3 bucks." Omar gave him the money. Leon went back in the store and returned with an issue of Fetish Times. "Here's your tour guide, good luck."

The Hellfire Club and The Vault were located in the decrepit meat packing district on and around 14th Street. Omar went to The Hellfire Club. It was $50 for a membership. Omar paid it. Much to his surprise, the place was clean. He introduced himself to Lenny, the manager, then gave Lenny his sales pitch.

"Seriously, a vampire," Lenny chuckled.

"Come over and see for yourself," Omar invited.

"Ain't gonna happen, partner, I'm gay, but I can send a representative."

"Fine, I'll get back to you when we're opening."

The Vault was a different story and cost Omar another $50 for a membership. A mistress was beating her slave while a dozen guys watched and jerked off. Everywhere Omar looked, guys were jerking off. They reminded Omar of the zombies in a George Romero movie. They watch a couple screwing, then wander off to watch another weird sex act. The scene creeped Omar out. He found a disinterested manager, gave him his pitch, then left. "I need to take a shower," he thought.

Omar had hired a manager/accountant, Jason. A stern looking short man who wore a three-piece suit and gold framed glasses. Omar found Jason waiting with a very important question.

"Now that you did your canvassing of the area, did you ever take into consideration of how you are going to feed her?"

"Feed her?"

"Yeah, it isn't like she's a lizard and can go months without food. She needs to be fed and that's going to be a major problem," Jason finished.

"Goddammit, you're right, I didn't think of that," Omar admitted. "Then how do we resolve this problem?"

"I need a sit down with some people."

"Do what you have to do," Jason told him, "but do it quick."

Omar made a call to a restaurant in Little Italy. He was to meet with a capo, Big Sal, who was his 'silent partner'. Omar explained that he could get rid of Sal's competition, permanently. "You call me, send them over, and no one will ever see them again." The two shook on the deal. Sal would send someone over to sample the merchandise and they never came back.

The Anchor had the sample the wares party. Gonzo and his three guys were offered a taste. Gonzo locked eyes with Lilith and backed off. This was nothing more than a rape, he felt. He was now questioning this arrangement. His guys didn't give a shit, hey free pussy was free pussy.

That would be their undoing. Gonzo wasn't the only one thinking the entire set up was wrong. Carol, the woman with tattoos from head to foot was having dreams about Lilith. Carol was 5'5" with short black hair and green eyes.

In her dreams, Lilith begged for help. "Free me," she moaned, "you must free me!" This was really getting to her; the place had been open for about six months and she had these dreams every night. Carol hung out with Gonzo as they both were potheads. She and Gonzo shared concerns that though even though business was great, something was very wrong.

"I see you and your friends don't talk much," she said to Gonzo.

"Fuck em', since Omar got them laid, they kiss his ass. I told Sandy that I think this deal is starting to suck, but he's getting paid, so all is well in his world."

"I think Omar is killing people."

"I don't think he is. I know he is, and he got my guys helping him dump the bodies." Gonzo stared at her for a minute.

"The smart move would be to let her go, but she'd kill us."

"Gonzo, I didn't tell you this, but she comes to me in my dreams. Every fuckin night she begs me to free her, but how can I?"

"I don't know, it's like opening a tiger's cage and trying to get away."

"I don't know about you, but sooner or later the hammer will fall. Omar advertised this place big time. He may be paying people to look the other way, but murder? It's going to backfire on him."

"Yeah, and my buddies are getting too used to the free pussy and nose candy."

"I don't want to be here when the shit goes down."

"Neither do I, but I have a bad feeling that if we do leave, we won't get too far."

"So that leaves us with..."

"Waiting for the first chance we get to jet the fuck outta here."

Omar had gotten heavily into coke. He had just done a couple of lines when he had some unwelcome visitors. Detectives Morelli and Muldoon requested to see the manager.

"What can I do for you gentlemen," Omar asked.

After showing their badges, Morelli spoke. "We are looking for some people, seems the last time they were seen was here."

"We get a pretty big crowd, any idea who they are?" Muldoon pulled out a handful of mug shots. "Anyone you know?" Actually, Omar knew all of them, he had fed them to Lilith.

"No, not really, but like I said, we get a lot of people through here."

Morelli handed Omar his card. "Any of them show up, I'd appreciate a call."

"No problem. Officer, we always cooperate with the police."

The two detectives left. Omar found Jason glaring at him.

"Might be time to rethink things," he told Omar.

"Why?"

"Because those two are the top vice cops in the city. They get a scent of something, they never let it go."

"I'm not worried."

"You should be and maybe you should back off on the coke, it's affecting your judgment."

"I can handle it just fine."

"You know, Omar, every coke head I ever met says the same thing."

"Hey, go fuck yourself and remember who pays you."

Jason shook his head and went back to his office.

Lilith had endured the constant rapes. They made a mistake in feeding her. Her strength was up, but she needed help. She had established a psychic connection with Carol. Carol was an outcast, but she had potential. The biker that didn't rape her was a possibility. She sensed his fear, but also respected that he didn't join in the abuse. One of them would free her, she would work on Carol.

Carol tried to sleep. Her conversation with Gonzo unnerved her. She knew he was right. Too many dollars at stake, they could never walk away and live. They knew that the others didn't. Omar was a stone killer and him getting into coke made him unstable and dangerous. Finally, she fell into a deep sleep.

Lilith reached out to her. "Carol is your name, right?"

"What do you want?"

"To be free of this place."

"I know, what they are doing isn't right. But I'm afraid of you, and them."

"You need not fear me, we can help each other, you know you are trapped here as I am."

"Strangely I had this same conversation."

"I know, I listened to it."

"How did you do that?"

"I'm not of your world, I'm not one of you, but you and I are similar. I have powers, but I'm restrained. Boldly put, free me, you live, don't you die, and I won't be your executioner. The bald man will be."

"The kingdom is crumbling."

"We both should not be here when it does. Think on what I said and sleep on it"

Lilith replayed the last six months over in her mind. Frat boys drooling on her as they spread her legs. The weight of fat, businessmen panting as they got off. Women perverts licking her, she hated the smell of them. But hated the bald man most of all. She would get revenge on all of them, she just had to wait for the girl to decide her fate.

Omar was doing coke in his office. One of the bikers, Denny, knocked on the door. "What do you want," Omar barked.

"Something you should know. I had to go see my parole officer and I overheard Morelli talking on the phone."

"And that means what to me?"

"They are getting a warrant to search the place."

"When?"

"That part I didn't hear, but it's gonna be soon." Omar tossed him an eight ball. "Thanks for telling me, I'll have to make some changes."

Omar thought he'd last longer, but yeah, changes need to be made. There was close to 500K in the safe, traveling money, he thought. Tonight, he would clean the safe out after hours and vanish. Maybe head south for a bit. Florida was prime territory. "Too bad I can't take my money maker with me," he thought.

Denny, loaded on coke, warned Gonzo and the others of the impending raid. Gonzo went looking for Carol. He found her outside, smoking a joint.

"If you're going to do something with that woman, do it now."

"Why, what's up?"

"A raid, that's what, I knew shit would come down after those two cops paid us a visit."

"We need to go"

"No shit, let her go, that's the diversion we need."

"Then you have to keep them occupied so they don't see me go to her."

"Ok, I have an idea, when you see me start yelling, make your move."

Gonzo went to Denny and slapped the coke out of his hand. He went off on what useless cocksuckers the three bikers had become. It got loud. Carol sneaked up the stairs. Entering the room, it smelled of stale blood and sex. The woman appeared to be sleeping. Carol unchained her and in a second, she was up and had Carol by the throat. "Everyone who hurt me must die," she growled. "Would you like to be like me," she seductively asked Carol.

"No, it's not what I want, I did what you asked, I want to go away from this place."

Lilith let her go. "I'm powerless until the sun goes down, I suggest that you take your friend and not be here by then."

"Thank you, we will be outta here shortly."

Carol went downstairs where things had escalated between Gonzo, the other bikers and now Omar. She got there in time to hear Gonzo bellow, "Fuck you, I quit!"

"You can't quit on me; I made a deal with your boss."

"The bullshit going on here broke any fuckin deal I made." Gonzo pulled a snub nosed .38 revolver out of his jacket. Omar put his arms up.

"Watch his arms," Carol yelled. "He has a derringer in his sleeve."

"Another fuckin traitor," Omar bellowed, but kept his hands up. "Carol, get behind me," Gonzo ordered. The two backed toward the door.

"This isn't over, you fuck, no one walks out on me, no one," Omar roared.

"Then I guess I should just blow you away," Gonzo said calmly. Omar paled at that.

"You two are walking dead," he snarled.

"Ya know what, open that fuckin safe, we need some back pay."

"Fuck you!"

Gonzo put his gun to Omar's head, "I don't think so, open it."

Omar spun the dial, opened the safe, then backed up.

"Help yourselves, you'll be dead by morning."

Gonzo kept the gun on Omar. "Carol, grab some cash and let's go."

Carol grabbed a couple of thick stacks of bills. Holding the gun on Omar, they backed out the door. "Now what," asked Carol.

"I need to make a call." Gonzo went to the first pay phone and called Sandy.

"The deal went bad; cops are coming and don't expect any of us back."

"What the fuck are you talking about," Sandy asked.

"Omar fucked us, that's all you need to know, so start covering your ass."

Gonzo hung up.

"What now," Carol asked.

"I need a drink, but not around here. Let's grab my bike and go downtown."

They rode into the heart of Times Square. Gonzo parked close to Club 44.

"It's a dive but it's safe," he told her. They ordered a couple of beers. "Let's just hang here until we hear something." The two drank quietly and watched the news on the crappy TV over the bar.

Omar was livid and cursing everyone out. It was after 6PM and the place was filling up. "Your fuckin buddy and Comic Strip Bitch are dead," Omar bellowed at the three remaining bikers. "Denny, I got a client who needs to go up top, you can take him up. The rest of you circulate." The 'client' was a stockbroker, a short fat man looking for thrills. Denny escorted him upstairs.

"Nice lamps," the guy remarked. "Yeah," said Denny, "the boss wanted that Goth look so he ran a gas line to these, pretty cool, right?"

"This is a classy place," the man remarked.

"Well wait 'till you see what you just bought." Denny opened the door and Lilith was waiting. She ripped Denny across the face with clawed hands. His eyes were destroyed. She grabbed the 'client' and ripped his throat out, drinking his spurting blood.

Denny staggered down the stairs screaming in agony. He stumbled into one of the fixtures, breaking it. Flames shot out and his greasy vest caught fire. Denny was now a living torch. People ran out of his way, but the fire was spreading. Then the cops arrived with a search warrant. But that was too late, the building was going up. Lilith walked through the chaos, killing with her claws and fangs. One of the remaining bikers pulled out a .25 automatic and shot her. She ripped his arm off and beat him to death with it.

Omar was in his office, cleaning out the safe when Jason arrived. "I knew you'd fuck us," Jason said. Jason had a .32 revolver pointed at

Omar. Omar flicked his arm and the derringer put a window in Jason's head. But Jason reflexively pulled the trigger and Omar took a bullet at the beltline.

"Son of a bitch," he bellowed, "things just ain't working out today." He packed the money in a metal briefcase.

The fire was out of control, the fire fighters were on their way. Lilith had just torn the head off the last biker. Torn up bodies littered the bar. Bleeding badly, Omar went to go out an emergency exit, but Lilith was blocking it. "Hey, I know you're pissed, but I'll split this cash with you." Lilith glared at him, she was covered with the blood of her victims. She would now get even. "Hey, it was just business, no reason to get uppity." He smirked. Lilith let out a horrific shriek and lunged for him.

Omar panicked, he threw the case at her head and turned to run. He felt a horrible pain as her hand sliced into his back and busted out of his chest in a shower of gore. He looked down and saw his heart in her bloody hand. She dropped it on the floor. Omar collapsed and crashed to the floor. Lilith took a long coat off a corpse and put it on. She joined the crowd outside the bar and watched it burn. Smiling, she walked away, never to be seen again.

Gonzo and Carol watched the bar burning during a news broadcast.

Gonzo turned to her and said, "I'm thinking Florida."

"Well, the weather is nice," she replied.

"Did you count that money?"

"Yeah, it a little over thirty thousand."

"That's a nice fresh start."

"Isn't it though."

"I say we leave now; you know someone will be wanting to talk to us."

"And we have nothing to say."

They finished their beers, topped off the fuel and headed down Interstate 95.

THE MUTT

The dog was big, dirty and roamed the area between 9th and 12th Avenues. He was a mix of German Shepard, Pit Bull and a dash of Lab thrown in. He had a big scar on his head where someone tried to do him in. He remembered being brought to these rotting piers and being left for dead. The dog didn't trust men as a man tried to kill him.

But he would forage for food by the meat packing plants on 14th Street. There his presence was tolerated. He became a mascot of sorts, menacing but never aggressive unless threatened. The dog weighed close to 150 lbs. He had no trouble with dog wardens as they rarely ventured into that area. He never ventured out of that area. This was his domain and he had friends there.

When night fell, his 'friends' ventured out. Low end street walkers and a couple of winos who enjoyed his company. To the girls, he was a protector of sorts. When the dog saw a pimp beating this girl called Lisa, it triggered a response. He was beaten by his master; he saw Lisa as a victim and acted accordingly. He bit the pimp on the ass. Not just a nip, he took a big chunk of meat out. Howling in pain, the pimp ran to the Emergency Ward at Saint Vincent's Hospital.

The whore, Lisa, and the dog bonded. Lisa would give him treats; the dog would shadow her while she worked. He lurked, out of sight, in the shadows of the Grey Hound Bus parking lot and in the ruins of the old post office. This is where the girls plied their trade. Burnt out drug casualties, they were giving blowjobs in the parked buses for $10. Some were independents, others still had a worthless pimp.

The Mutt seemed aware that a Cadillac coming into this area was trouble. He would watch these people, set to pounce if any girl was attacked. It was like he was a sheep dog, and these hookers were his flock. But there was an incident where he saved a guy's life. That guy put the word out, "Fuck with that dog and you'll answer to me." So, the dog roamed the area and wasn't bothered.

Tonight, the dog was watching Lisa. Lisa was a skinny woman with dirty blonde hair. She wore a pink tube top and pink mini skirt. She allowed herself to get past the stage where she could work in a house or massage parlor. She didn't have a pimp, but one was very interested in getting her and others into his 'stable'. None of the women wanted that, it was hard enough getting $10 for a blowjob. Splitting that wouldn't leave them much, but this pimp, Troy, wasn't giving up easily.

Troy was a nobody who wanted to be somebody. He was a skinny, black guy with bad teeth. He dressed the part in a cheap imitation, fur coat and leopard print wide hat. He wasn't liked, in fact he was barely tolerated. Most places threw him out as he was a loudmouth and a dust head. Angel dust, aka PCP became his drug of choice. But it also made him violent when things didn't go quite the way he wanted.

Tonight, he wanted money. He used the last of his cash for some dust. He was going to grab a bitch. In his burnt brain, it was his time. So, he drives down to 9th Avenue, by the Greyhound Station. Girls would sneak a john into one of the buses and do him there. He parked and waited; a predator ready to pounce. His brain was on fire, but his purpose clear.

Lisa walked with Nadine, a chunky black girl with a huge Afro. The night had been very slow, so they wanted to change locations. "Always more action by the bus lot," Lisa commented.

"Shit girl tonight has been deader than an old man's dick, I needs to earn."

"Tell me about it," Lisa replied. The Mutt walked a respectable distance behind them.

Troy stepped out between two parked vans.

"Goin' out," Nadine asked.

Troy grabbed her, "No yous goin with me." Lisa slung her purse at Troy's head. Troy ducked then punched her in the face. The Mutt launched at Troy, but Troy swung a van door open, and the Mutt ran into it. Troy shoved Nadine into his car, smashing her head on the door frame. The Mutt was down and dazed. Troy kicked him in the side and looked at Lisa. She was trying to get up. He spit at her, then drove away. The Mutt struggled to his feet.

He went over to Lisa, whose lip was split and bleeding. He licked her face and she used him to get to her feet. She leaned against a van. "That cocksucker, that rotten cocksucker, what the fuck, where did he go?" The Mutt looked at her, then looked in the direction Troy went. He sniffed the air and trotted off. He hurt, but not enough to stop him. He went hunting.

Troy was oblivious to the fact that Nadine was half conscious and bleeding heavily from a gash on her head. Troy talked nonstop about his plans before he noticed his potential source of income might be dying. He shook her shoulder and she groaned. He slapped her face and came away with bloody hands. "I'll sell her, that's what I'll do, I'll sell her to the porn guys." He parked in the middle of 42nd Street.

The Mutt wound up on the corner of 8th Avenue and 42nd Street. He sniffed the air. His ears went up. He slowly walked up the right side of the block. He passed The Anco Theater, Athena Liquors, 250 Book Center, Courageous Books, The Rialto Theaters, Hubert's Museum, The Liberty Theater and Blackjack Books. He sniffed the air again and snarled. His quarry was in Blackjacks.

Tonawanda Pete, the night manager, and Leon, the bouncer, were discussing the upcoming wrestling matches this coming Monday at the Garden. "Bruno will kick that fuckin Commie's ass, I'm willing to bet on it," Pete said.

"That Koloff's a tough motherfucker, should be a good fight," Leon added. "Yeah, let's get .... What the hell is he doing?" Troy barged in dragging a bloody Nadine.

"Get the fuck out of here, get her to a hospital," yelled Pete.

"I want to sell her, how much you gimmie?"

"Are you deaf? Get her out of here."

"Call yo boss, I needs me some cash, give me a hundred for her."

"Leon, call the cops, fuck this shit."

"Don't you be touching that phone, I'll cut choo." Troy pulled out a razor.

Troy lunged, both men backed up. The Mutt walked in. Troy didn't notice. The Mutt lunged in and ripped open Troy's leg. He shook Troy like he was a rag doll. Blood shot out in an arc. The Mutt tore the femoral artery to shreds. The Mutt dropped Troy. Customers stared in disbelief.

"Leon, call the cops," Pete ordered. Then he ran to the back of the store and opened a door that led to an alley. That alley ran behind all the building on the block. "Dog, get," Pete yelled. "Everybody get the fuck out lessen you want to talk to the man." There was a rush to the door.

"Leon, they came in here like this, all fucked up, let's get the story straight."

"It's like you said, Boss, they came in here all ripped up, must have been a mugging."

"Yeah, and this was such a nice neighborhood and all that."

The Mutt slunk down the alley slowly. He heard sirens. He hid behind a dumpster for a bit. Then he worked his way down to 8th Avenue. He walked past some shoeshine stands. "That's one bloody ass dog," one of the bootblacks remarked. He stayed out of sight until he found Lisa.

"What did you do?" She looked at him, horrified. The Mutt just looked at her, wagging his tail.

"You musta got Troy, I got to get you cleaned up." She took the Mutt to the station and found a spigot they used to wash out the buses. She hosed the blood off the Mutt. The Mutt shook the bloody water off him. A few days later, Nadine returned with a bandage on her head.

"I was in the hospital; I don't remember anything after Troy grabbed me. The police say we was mugged, and Troy, he's dead," Nadine told her.

"You didn't get mugged, I don't know what happened, but the dog saved your ass," Lisa told her.

Nadine looked at the Mutt and the Mutt just wagged his tail.

"Our protector," she sighed. "He's a good dog."

RETRIBUTION

The room stank of blood, shit, piss and death. My ruined body is propped up in a chair. I am dead, though for whatever reason, I linger. I fucked up, I picked up the wrong trick. The bastard was smart. He takes his victims to a long-abandoned building down on 9th avenue. The area was a no man's land of the depraved. Transsexual hookers, junkies, and the insane homeless people.

Me? I was a hooker, a hooker of the lowest kind. The drugs that numbed me to my trade were my undoing. I was so low that I'd take $5 to blow a guy in his car. Because of my habit, I was down to under 100 pounds. But did I deserve what happened? Did I deserve to be raped and tortured for days? To have bottles and chair legs shoved into my pussy and asshole? To be burned with a lit cigarette, to be almost strangled to death only to be brought back so he could have more 'fun'? I don't think so.

My body is broken, cut up and ready to be discarded. He will look for more prey. So why am I still here? I don't get it, I wished for death, for release from the pain and terror. I look at this rotten bastard and what he has done. I'm not the first, he's been doing this for the last few months. I don't think the cops care about dead hookers. They view girls like me as a nuisance. We are an easy bust. But now we are easy prey for who they are calling The Times Square Ripper.

Joe Costa was a drunk. Joe oversaw a Fortune 500 company at one time. But years of liquid lunches caught up with him. He was let go and being let go sent him into a downward spiral. Waking up in an alley or alcove in his own piss and puke was a common thing for Joe. Try as he may to straighten out, his addiction kept him in the gutter.

Joe got on disability, but he'd drink that up before the first week of the month was up. At one time, Joe looked like a younger version of Dean Martin. Now he had the emaciated, bloated look of an alcoholic. Joe would shoplift hair tonic and cough syrup for its alcohol content.

Joe gets the Dt's and hallucinates sometimes. With nowhere to go, Joe is just walking, no destination in mind. Tonight, he is on 9th Avenue, just wandering.

 I called myself Candy, I was sweet as candy five years ago, but now I'm a slab of butchered meat. I don't know why I'm still here. Is it possible to stop this killer? I don't know how. I can drift away from here, but not too far, something is holding me here. I know he's out there hunting, he had me for five days. He might be satisfied for the moment, but he's never really satisfied. I saw it in his eyes, he won't stop, he must be stopped.

 The killer walked down 42nd Street. He was, for the moment, satisfied. The whore lasted longer than he thought she would. He enjoyed her screams, her moans of pain, her begging for it to end. It ended like the rest of them, a dead whore that the cops wouldn't bother investigating. There will be more, as soon as the urge came to him, he would hunt.

 There was nothing special about him that anyone would notice. He was white, in his mid-30's, a slightly stocky build and a baby face. That face is what got them, it was goofily innocent. He blended in the area well as out of towners would come in from Jersey, Brooklyn, Staten Island, even as far as the New England states. Yeah, he fit in well with the Chicken Hawks, toilet queens, peepshow regulars and perverts in general.

 He knew eventually he'd get caught. They would blame his behavior on reading 50's pinup and bondage magazines. They would say he had 'mommy' issues. They would blame his crimes on everything but the truth. The truth was that he was born bad, he liked to cause pain, and he hid that from his parents. Any pet that he was given vanished in about a week. He'd say the pet ran away. He lied. He tortured and killed his kittens, then a puppy.

 The truth was that he didn't like anyone, but men were two strong for him to take on. He did try to take off a transsexual hooker. But the hooker scared him, she was big and put up too much of a fight. He ran from her. She made him feel weak. He didn't like that feeling. His first was easy. A street walker down on 9th avenue. He didn't wash for a week, he wanted to see how a whore would react. Well, this whore gagged at the stench of him when he fished his cock out for a blowjob. She backed away and he hit her. He caved in her head with a brick for disrespecting him. He beat her head to a bloody pulp, then dumped her in the Hudson River. The blue crabs, turtles and fish feasted. She was never found or missed. He went home and masturbated, thinking of the kill. This was just a taste of the horror to come to 42nd Street.

He was ready to hunt again. Hookers were getting too easy, he wanted a challenge, someone new to abuse and discard. He decided to cruise the arcades, like Fascination and Playland. These places were infested with pedos and chicken hawks. Young black and Hispanic boys would sell themselves to get movie money. It was a sick, slimy scene. The killer fit right in.

Candy saw Joe roaming around. She decided to try and get his attention. "Joe," she said.

Joe's head jerked up. "Who the fuck is there," he muttered, confused.

"Joe, it's Candy." "Where you at, lady, I don't see you."

"Joe, you can't see me because I'm dead."

"If you're dead, how come I can hear you?"

"How the fuck should I know, but Joe, you gotta listen to me."

"It's the booze talking, go away"

"It's not the fuckin booze, just listen to me."

"You're for real?"

"Yeah, Joe, I'm a fuckin ghost and you gotta help."

"What can I do if you're dead?"

"Stop my murderer, that's what."

"How do I do that?"

"You wait here, that building across the street is his place, he'll go there."

"Then what?"

"You call the cops."

"I can do that."

"Good, now we wait."

"You sure you're dead, I mean maybe this is the booze making me think I hear you."

Candy thought on this. "Joe, stick your hand out."

"Why?"

"I want to try something."

"Ok." Joe Stuck his hand out, Candy took it. "Goddamn, that's fuckin cold."

"You believe me now?" "Yeah, I guess so, now what?"

"We wait, he'll be back, and you will have to stop him."

"I'm not that brave."

"You're going to have suck it up, buddy." "Ah fuck me, he really hurt you bad?"

"I'm fuckin dead, Joe, it don't get any badder than that." "We wait then."

Joe searched around a pile of shattered concrete and found a long piece of rebar.

"Might need this," he muttered. "Cave his fuckin' skull in with it."

"I need a drink."

"No, you need to keep watch with me."

"What if he don't show?"

"You come back tomorrow night."

"Why me?"

"Because you can hear me, for whatever reason, you can hear me." "I want to see what he did to you."

"No, you really don't."

"Yeah, I do, if I'm going to do this, I need to see why."

"Second floor, building across the street, hold your nose or you'll puke."

Joe enters the building, the stench of something rotten hits him. He walks to the 2nd floor. He sees what is left of Candy. A terrible rage overcomes him. He storms out. "Candy, where are ya?"

"I'm here, Joe"

"I'm gonna kill that fucker, graveyard dead." "That's the spirit."

"I gotta take a piss."

As Joe went to water the lilies, the killer had picked out his prey. He spotted the two girls at PIA, a store that sold fake Ids, weapons, badges, and porn. They were getting fake Ids obviously to go clubbing. They could be about 15-16 years old. One was a slim blonde, the other a pudgy red head. He had never done two before. His inner demons screamed in his mind. He bet himself he could make them last a week. He felt himself getting hard. Now to make a move.

He stood close to Athena Liquors. When they passed him, he said loudly, "Good smoke, I got good smoke, you buying?"

The blonde asked, "Any good?"

"Sweety, I gots Columbian Gold, primo shit, girl."

"Cool, how much?"

"I'll give you a quarter oz for $50."

"That's a lot of bread."

"Yeah, but it's Gold, baby. Tell you ladies what, I'll give you a taste."

"Ok, sounds good, twist one up."

"No, not here, too many eyes on us, I got a place close by."

"Where?"

"Not far, Ninth avenue, real private." The two girls talked for a minute.

"Ok, we'll go, but no funny stuff."

"I'm just a weed dealer, just looking to make some cash."

"Well, let's get going then."

He led the girls down 42nd street to 9th Avenue. Candy saw him approaching with the girls. "Sweet Jesus, they are just children, Joe, where the fuck are you?" Joe, after pissing, sat down and nodded out. The killer stopped in front of the decrepit building. "You really live here," the redhead asked.

"Yeah, why, you don't like it?"

"No, it's creepy, I'm not going in."

"You'll spoil the party."

"We came to score weed, not to party with you."

"Now you're pissing me off."

"Hey, fuck you, I told you no funny stuff."

The killer pulled out a curved utility knife. He grabbed the blonde and held the blade against her cheek. Then he cut her.

"Get inside or I'll peel her face off."

The redhead tried to run. He tripped her, then kicked her in the side. The blonde is holding her bloody face, crying. He grabbed both girls, who are now in shock, and forced them in the building.

Candy finds Joe passed out. Her rage becomes a tangible thing. She slaps him. Her hand passes through his face, but he stirs.

"Joe, get the fuck moving, he's here and he has two kids." Joe staggers to his feet. "Move your ass, Joe, he's going to start cutting on them."

Joe wipes his hand over his face, picks up the piece of rebar and heads into the building.

The killer is beating on the girls, trying to knock them out so he can tie them up. The redhead is putting up too much of a fight. He punches her in the face, breaking her nose. She goes down in a heap. He starts cutting the blonde's clothes off. He pulls her pants off and drools. "Nice pink little pussy, I'll open it up a bit." He goes to use his knife when the door flies open. Joe cracks the rebar across his arm, breaking it with a wet snap.

"Get out of here and call the cops," he yells at the girls. Helping each other stand, they stagger out of the building. Candy sees them. "Good, they are getting away. What's Joe doing in there?" Joe is facing a very pissed off psycho.

"You ruined everything, you're gonna pay for that." His right arm was broken about the wrist.

"No, asshole, you're just about done, listen." There were sirens blaring as two cop cars sped down 9th Avenue. The killer knew he was screwed. "Don't move," Joe told him. Joe took his eyes off the killer for one second and got kicked in the balls. The killer ran for the door.

"Nooo," Candy screamed. She had been watching the scene play out. Her rage became a force. As the killer reached the door, it slammed him in the face, knocking him loopy. Joe staggered over and fell on top of him.

Joe dropped heavy fists to the back of the guy's head. Then the cops charged in.

They didn't know who was who. The girls identified Joe as their savior. The killer was rushed to The Tombs and held without bail. Joe was hailed as a hero.

Joe led them to Candy's remains. "She needs a decent burial," Joe explained. His request for a decent burial wasn't going anywhere. But a sympathetic mortician offered to cremate the remains. Joe agreed to that. Joe took Candy's ashes and went back to 9th Avenue.

"I don't know if you can hear me, but I owe you. I got you in this urn and I'm going to scatter your ashes here so maybe you'll be at peace." Candy watched as her ashes were scattered by the wind. Joe walked away and got his life together. Candy's spirit stayed in that area. She haunted those decaying buildings, scaring off predators looking to harm anyone.

"I guess this is punishment for my past life," she thought. She watched the progression of change going on. Then someone decided to demolish that entire block. Candy watched the wrecking ball take down the site of her murder. She felt a change. "I'm free now," she realized, then went off to where we go as we eventually are all lost to the ravages of time.

TEDDY'S PLACE

1

Teddy G was a made man. At 60, he wanted to take over a bar, Club 45, and relax a bit. It was 1977, things were opening up that hadn't been opened up before. Teddy was a big bear of a man, his taking over the bar would put him in the heart of Times Square. An ideal location for keeping an eye on certain 'family' investments. Teddy needed help changing this over, he needed a fixer, he needed Vince Toricelli.

I get a call that Teddy G wants a word. I tell him I'll be at the Club 45 at noon. I get there, the place is still advertising that Midnight Cowboy and The Owl and the Pussycat had scenes shot in there. Teddy is sitting in the back. He is talking to a guy who has something to do with the jukebox. The guy was skinny with granny glasses and bell bottom jeans.

"I don't want any of that hippie shit in there."

"You won't get much play then."

"I don't give a shit, put in Dino, Frank, Tony Bennett, The Four Seasons, the Beatles..."

"I don't have any of that stuff."

"Well, you're going to have to find it now, aren't you?"

I saw the kid had his balls up, so it was time for me to 'fix' it. "Teddy, let me talk to the kid, I'll set him straight."

"Vince, you better do it before I do."

"You," I said, "let's go for a walk." I took the kid outside.

"What's your name?"

"Jack."

"Jack, I'm Vince and we have a problem."

"Yeah, that old bastard isn't letting me do what I get paid to do."

"Jack, that old bastard can put you in the ground if you piss him off. It's his place, he wants his music in his jukebox. He doesn't care about how many plays any record gets, he wants what he wants, and I make sure he gets it."

Jack looked like he was going to cry.

"I don't have any of those records, they are too old."

"You want to be a hero?"

"What do you mean?"

"Wouldn't both our lives be easier if you went the extra mile for Teddy?"

"I guess, but like I said, I don't have those tunes."

"But you understand what he wants, right?"

"Yeah, I guess he wants oldies."

I slapped Jack on the back. "Now we are talking and I'm gonna help you." Vince peeled off five twenties. "Take this and go to Entertainment Outlet on 14th street. They have bins of 45's, lots of oldies. Get a load of them and fill the juke with some then give the rest to Teddy to switch around."

"I can do that," said Jack, "you want me to spend the whole hundred?"

"If you find enough tunes to cover it, why not? That way I'm happy, Teddy's happy and you made a very important friend."

"Ok, thanks, Vince, I'll be back tomorrow with whatever I find."

"Good lad, that's the spirit. See you then."

I go back inside.

Teddy looks up, "Well?"

"I explained it to him, I think he's a good kid. Joey probably has some tunes he wants pushed, so I'll tell him your juke is off limits."

"Fuck Joey, I'll tell him that myself."

Joey was Joe Gallo, a rather loose cannon that no one wanted to cross. I kept my mouth shut.

"Vince, I want all that crap gone." Teddy points to the Midnight Cowboy sign. "Last thing I want in here is tourists."

"You want to close up for a couple of days while we do some work?"

"No, I think I want to see who frequents this place, I might have to eighty-six some people."

"Teddy, you know I work the area and I'll tell you honestly that this place doesn't draw much traffic."

"Really? Well then, I want you to tell people you know that are all right that Teddy's is open for business."

• • • •

2

I WASN'T LYING, CLUB 45 was a dead bar. The Midnight Cowboy thing brought in curious tourists, but that movie was in '69, close to ten years ago. No one gave a shit anymore. I knew what Teddy wanted; he wanted a place to hold court. But he also wanted friendly barflies to make the place work. Two likely candidates were Nails Morgan and Cueball Jones.

An odd couple as Morgan was a burly white guy with a scarred-up forehead. Jones was a slick black dude with a shaved head. They did 'jobs' together, but they made some good scores a few months ago and were flush. The fact that almost an entire block burned to the ground, well, I'm not supposed to know anything about that.

I found them at one of their usual haunts, McGirr's Pool Hall. "Gentlemen, how's tricks?"

"Well, look who's here, Vicious Vince himself. How's it hanging, hump," Nails inquired.

"I'm good, gents, real good. Got a new place to quench your thirsts," Vince informed them.

"And what might this new place have to offer serious drinkers like ourselves," Jones asked.

"Teddy G just bought Club 45. Now it's Teddy's Place."

"Damn, I heard Teddy say he was headed to Florida to bask in retirement sunshine."

"That may happen down the road, Teddy has business interests here, so he's in semi-retirement."

"Teddy put a few people in the ground, but that was his job. Teddy always treated us right," Nails added.

"Exactly, that's why you'd be welcome there. You'd be a deterrent as to potential problems."

"What's the joint got to offer," Jones asked.

"Well Teddy is loading the juke box with some old tunes and is going to hire a couple of cute barmaids."

"That sounds a lot better than what it was. They've been pushing that Midnight Cowboy crap for the last ten years. When is the grand opening?"

"Soon I would think. I just sent the juke box guy to pick up tunes that Teddy likes."

"Ok, we'll be there, just let us know when the big day is."

"We'll bring cannolis, I know Teddy likes his pastries," Nails added.

"I'm thinking Saturday, today is only Monday, so mark that date on your dance calendar," Vince told them.

Vince knew that Morgan and Jones were stand up guys and would be good to have around. He went back to the club and saw Jack struggling with a bunch of boxes.

"How did you make out," Vince asked.

"I hit a home run, but these fucken boxes are heavy."

"I'll give you a hand." Jack had six good-sized boxes filled with records.

"You know what, stay here, Teddy must have a hand truck in there." Vince went inside.

"Teddy, I need a hand truck."

"What for?"

"Jack just came back with a shitload of records."

"There's one in the stock room, hope that kid got the right stuff."

Jack and Vince piled six boxes on the hand truck. They pulled them into the bar and dropped them in front of Teddy. Teddy gave Jack a sort of dirty look.

"Let's see whatcha got here kid." Teddy sifted through the records.

Dean Martin, The Four Seasons, The Supremes, The Four Tops, Frank Sinatra, Tony Bennett, The Beach Boys, The Beau Brummels, The Yardbirds, The Kingsmen, Bobby Fuller Four, The Standels, Charley Pride, Johnny Cash, the Drifters, The Temptations, Stevie Wonder and more.

"More of the same in all these boxes," Teddy asked Jack.

"Yeah, pretty much so," Jack told him. Jack took a twenty out and handed it to Vince.

"I got it all for eighty," Jack told him. "Here's your change."

"Keep it, you done good."

"Yeah," said Teddy. "You done real good, kid, Lenny, give Jack here a drink."

Lenny was Teddy's bartender, but also was his bodyguard. Lenny was 6' 2" 250 pounds of muscle and had hands the size of small hams.

"Kid," Teddy said. "I'll need you to come in once a month and switch some of these around."

"Sure, Teddy, be happy to do it."

Jack sat at the bar with his beer chatting with Lenny. Vince watched Teddy go through a box and he was smiling.

"Now this is music," Teddy said to no one in particular.

"Vince, I want to hire a manager, someone to take care of the day-to-day business."

"You got Lenny."

"Yeah, but I need him for other things, plus he's not a people person."

"I would have never guessed." Both men chuckled at that, drawing a dirty look from Lenny.

"You know anyone who you think would work out?"

Vince pondered that a minute. "I might have someone, but right now she's at The Retreat."

"She's a hooker? Don't want hookers working out of here, that would get us into a jackpot."

"Teddy, did you ever know me to drag trash into our business? Yeah, right now she's working there, she got a raw deal with a shitbag ex-husband and a sick mother. Plus, she's one of us. I moved her there because I felt she deserved better."

"She's Italian?"

"Yes sir, she certainly is."

"And this isn't like you're trying to get into her pants?"

"No Teddy, nothing like that. I respect her, she has balls and takes no shit. I put her in a better spot, I can put her here if you trust my judgement."

Teddy frowned and thought about it. "You think she's special, don't you?"

"I said I respect her grit. Would I bang her? No, not unless something happened between us. I don't let pussy sidetrack me, never have, never will."

"Then I need to meet her. Bring her around tomorrow."

"How about around noon?"

"That will be perfect."

• • • •

3

VINCE WAS HOPING THAT this wouldn't be a mistake. Sure, he liked Connie, she was a tough broad. That long brown hair, an ass that won't quit and those green eyes burned a hole in you. He had to make sure that she was right for the job. Vince took a cab to The Retreat and told the driver to wait. Bruno, the owner was in his office.

"Bruno, how's business," Vince asked.

"Right now, kind of slow. Summer months and all that. People are going on vacations, not screwing."

"Did you hear that Teddy G just took over Club 45?"

"No, I didn't, but good for him. I love Teddy, he's a stand-up guy."

"He's looking for a manager for the place."

Bruno stood up. "Let me guess, you want to put Connie there."

"Will that create a problem for you and me?"

"No, not really. She's a good kid, but we both know she's better than this. Plus, she intimidates some of the guys. She's in control and strong and they don't like that."

"So, if Teddy wants to hire her, no problem?"

"She'll have my blessing if she wants to better herself."

"Thanks, Bruno, I didn't want to create a problem for you."

"She's in the back, are you taking her to meet the Big Guy?"

"Yeah, it's his call, I just suggested that she may be what he wants."

"Let me know either way how it works out."

Vince went back where the dressing room was. Connie was reading The Daily News. She looked at Vince and smiled. "Well, if it isn't my knight in dented armor. What's up Sir Vincent?"

Vince pulled out a chair and sat down. "Remember I told you that if I found you a better situation would you take a chance on it.?"

"Vince, promises, promises, but you did get me out of that shithole and set me up here. So, I'll listen, talk to me," Connie said.

"Ok, this could be a ticket to better things, or you may just tell me to go fuck myself."

"What's the job, sucking more cocks?"

"Actually, not sucking anything. Do you think you can manage a bar?"

Connie thought about it. "Is it a strip bar or something?"

"No, it's Club 45, Teddy G took it over. It will be his hangout. He wants a manager and I thought of you."

"No turning tricks? No bullshit?"

"None of that, listen to me, Teddy will test you, give it right back to him, he's like that. Now get dressed in something casual and we go have a sit down."

Connie put on a black t-shirt and tight blue jeans. Her green eyes sparkled. What's the worst that could happen, he'll say no?

"Trust me when I tell you that if he goes for it, you'll be taken care of."

"I trusted you once and you helped me, so I'm putting my trust in you again, something I rarely do with a man." They went outside and got in the cab.

Teddy was holding court in the back of the bar. Nails Morgan was there and so was a box of Italian pastries. "Nails, you may be an ugly bastard, but you have great taste in pastries."

"Thanks, Teddy, coming from a half dead made man, that's a great compliment."

Lenny almost spit out his teeth.

"Lively bunch," Connie said as they approached the table.

"Well Nails, I see you're already trying to ingratiate yourself here."

"Vince," Teddy said over a mouthful of something. "The man knows his pastries, even better, he knows the ones I like."

"Where's your swarthy sidekick today?"

"Jonesy has a new lady, so he's over her place spending some quality time."

Vince motioned toward Connie. "Teddy, this is the lady I told you about, Connie, Teddy, Teddy, Connie." Teddy stood up and shook her hand.

"Vince thinks very highly of you, and I think very highly of Vince, so you get points. But how bad do you want the job, bad enough to take care of Teddy?"

"No disrespect Mr. Teddy, but me 'taking care of you' would probably put you in traction or the emergency room."

Teddy got a hard look on his face as he stared her down. Then he burst out laughing.

"You took it, and you threw it back, I like that. Now to business. I need you to run this place, be the public face of it. You won't get any shit as people will always be here. You dress nice, sexy, they can look, but not touch. Be nice, but tough when you have to be. I'll teach you how to do the books, order the booze, and run the help. Do you know how to tend bar?"

"No but I'll, learn."

"Good, I'll hire another bartender and a couple of barmaids. I don't want any crap going on in here, no hustling, no dealing. You see any of the help doing that, they are gone. You get $500 cash a week. You're off Monday and Wednesday. I'm gonna run a card game in the back. You work that too. You'll double that $500 in tips. So, do we have a deal?"

Connie was speechless. Vince spoke for her. "She'll take it Teddy."

"Let her talk for herself," Teddy said.

"Yes," Connie said, "I'll take it and thank you, I won't let you down."

"We'll see about that, I want you to work with Lenny today, he'll show you the basics. If you want to try a bartender's school, I can make that happen too."

"I can show her everything she needs to know. It ain't like we are making drinks with those little fuckin umbrellas here."

"So, show her already," Teddy told Lenny.

• • • •

4

DOWN THE ASS END OF 42nd Street, four guys were in a cheap hotel smoking PCP. Thugs and lowlifes, they weren't welcome anywhere. Paco Sanchez was 28 and had been a junkie since he was 15 years old.

He had a lengthy record for robbery, assault and rape. He was painfully thin with a pockmarked face. Willie Leary was 35, short with red hair and freckles. He used to run with The Westies, but he burned them on deals and wasn't welcome in Hell's Kitchen anymore. Burt Topper was white trash, he liked robbing and beating up street walkers. At 45, he was the oldest of the bunch. He was heavily tattooed as he was in the HA but was stripped of his colors for stealing. Smoking PCP made him violent. Last of the group was Armand, a Haitian who had a terrible case of body odor. Another druggie, the crap leaked out of his pores.

The four were broke, they grabbed this room when a hooker left after turning a trick. Paco had rounded them up as he needed a big score, something that would keep them in drugs for weeks. But they were too well known. If one tried to go into a bookstore, they wouldn't get passed the counter. Tonowanda Pete, the Night Manager of Blackjack Books, had personally beaten the shit out of Willie and Paco for trying to shoplift.

"We need some heavy green to get more sherm," Paco told them.

"No shit," said Burt. "We can't do nothing around here, especially on The Deuce. Marty and John's boys won't let us go into anything there."

"Den we gotta branch out, go where no one would tink we are up to something," Armand added.

"I might have a job we can do," Willie said. "Really, like what," Paco asked.

"New place is having a grand opening Saturday. The big wop, Teddy, bought Club 45. They are having a big shindig. If we wander in about an hour before they close, there should be a lot of cash."

"Yeah, that's a great idea, those eye ties are all about cash," replied Paco. "At 3am they won't be expecting anything. We go in, throw down on them, clean the place out, then get the fuck outta here. You guys in?"

"We all need guns, dem wops will be packin'," Armand added.

"How many of us got a piece," Paco asked. Willie and Burt had .38 pistols, Paco has a 45 automatic, Armand had nothing.

"Three is better than nothing, Armand can watch the door and keep anyone from bothering us. So, do we have a plan?"

They were all in. "Saturday night, we meet on the corner of 45th and 8th, then we do the job," Paco finished. The four went their separate ways.

• • • •
5

CONNIE WAS A QUICK study. Lenny taught her the basics, but she went to Strand's Books and picked up The Bartender's Standard Manual by Fred Powell. They cleaned the place up. All the Midnight Cowboy signs were tossed out. They didn't last long on the curb. Scavengers took them, they probably wound up at a flea market. Vince made the rounds, inviting people to Teddy's Grand Opening. It would be a who's who of high-lifes and low-lifes.

Vince lured two barmaids from another bar, Lisa and Candy. Lisa was a tall blonde with legs that never quit and a 38 D chest. Candy was an Asian lady with long, black hair and a toned body. Both worked as high-end call girls during the day. Lenny would hang around as a bouncer until they found another guy. Lenny put a sawed-off double-barreled shotgun under the bar.

"Just in case, cause ya never know," he told Vince.

Saturday was the big day. Teddy was respected and feared, so the boys came out to wish him luck on his new venture. Connie circulated, joked with the patrons and pushed drinks. Lisa and Candy hustled and were raking in the tips. Teddy had a table in the back and held court. Joe Bikini stopped in, as did Marty Hodas, Eddie Miskin and others in the skin trade. Even Crazy Joe Gallo showed up and mended fences with Teddy. Around midnight, two not so welcome 'guests' arrived.

Detectives Sal Morelli and Brian Muldoon worked vice. Morelli was the more laid back of the two. Muldoon was a head breaker with no class. He hated the area and was a racist and a bully. Morelli was stuck with him. Muldoon liked to bait people. He walked up to Teddy's table. "Hey Teddy, do you know why they don't like helicopters to fly over Italy?

"No, but I'm sure you're going to tell me," Teddy replied.

"It's cause the big ones go wop, wop, wop, and the little ones go ginnie, ginnie, ginnie." Muldoon cracked up as storm clouds gathered on Teddy's face.

"Hey Muldoon," Vince said. "Do you know why Irishmen always sing about their mothers?"

Muldoon turned to him and said, "I don't want to hear it."

"It's because they don't know who their fathers are," Vince finished. Muldoon's face turned beet red.

"Calm down, big guy, you look like you're going to have a stroke," Vince said.

"I'm going to kick your wop ass right now," Muldoon bellowed.

"You're gonna try, and considering last time you got 'tough', Blackjack's night manager kicked your ass."

"You're a dead man," roared Muldoon, but Morelli pulled him back. "That's right, stick up for your greasy buddies," Muldoon screamed at him. "I'm done with you; Monday I'm asking for a new partner." Muldoon stormed out.

Sal said, "Vince, let him get another partner, he's an asshole and he's gonna go down. I'd hate to see him take you with him."

"You're right, I'm so tired of his shit and covering for him. Teddy, I apologize for him."

"Sorry, Sal, that won't cut it after this. I want his fat ass back here with hat in hand," Teddy told him.

Morelli just nodded then left. Teddy snorted. "If I could make that prick vanish without problems…"

"No, Teddy, we can't go there," Vince said. "Let Sal handle it; you know there are lines we can't cross."

"That cocksucker pisses me off. Too bad Pete didn't cripple him," Teddy said. Just then, Tondawanda Pete came in. Pete was the night manager of Blackjack Books. A Vietnam vet and all around badass, Pete beat the shit out of Muldoon a couple of months ago. Had Morelli not stopped it, Pete would have put Muldoon in the hospital.

"Well look who's here, taking the night off," asked Teddy.

"Not really," said Pete. "Leon can handle it for a couple of hours, I just wanted to come over for your grand opening."

"You just missed your old pal, Muldoon," Vince told him.

"I saw him come in, so I waited. I think he'd put a bullet in me if he could get away with it."

"Fuck him, he's a piece of shit. Have a drink with me, Pete," Teddy told him.

• • • •

6

AROUND 2:30AM, THE 'crew' met on the corner of 45th Street and 8th Avenue. Paco and Burt were the first ones there. They smoked a joint full of angel dust. Willie Leary had been drinking all day, but he could handle it, or so he said. Armand was the last to arrive. "I got me a piece," he told them. Armand showed them a .22 pistol, aka A Saturday Night Special. Burt looked at it and laughed. "That piece of junk might blow up in your hand," he chuckled.

"It's fine," Paco snarled, the PCP was firing him up. "He's watching the door, so anyone tries to get in, he can shoot them." Another PCP laden joint was passed around. All four were nervous and that didn't bode well. PCP was a shitty drug that induced psychosis and sometimes superhuman strength. Guys whacked out on it could snap off handcuffs. Paco finally said "ok, let's go do this thing."

At the same time Morelli caught up to Muldoon. "Brian, you really crossed a line with Teddy."

"Like I give a fuck about that goomba grease ball."

"He wants an apology."

"Hell will freeze over before he gets one."

"Ok, you and I are done. I can't work with you anymore. You're pissing the wrong people off. So, this is what I'll do. We go apologize to Teddy. Then Monday, we go see the chief and tell him to split us up."

"Ya know Sal, I'm sick of you too. You kiss up to these scumbags and I'm tired of it. I want a partner that will have my back. Not like you. So ok, I'll suck hind tit just to get rid of you." They started walking back to Teddy's.

As fucked up as they were, the four entered the bar singly. Paco went up to the bar. Willie was close to Teddy's table. Burt took a seat close to where Nails and Jones were chatting up Lisa. Armand took a position by the door. He locked it. Lenny saw him do it and yelled, "Hey asshole, unlock that fuckin door and get out of here." The three pulled their guns out.

"Give us what we want and none of yas get hurt", Paco yelled. "Bitch, empty the register."

"Empty it yourself, you spic bastard." Paco shot her in the face.

"Noooo", Vince screamed. Paco turned and shot him in the shoulder. Vince fell behind the bar. Willie takes a shot at Teddy, but Lenny pushes Teddy into the back room and takes a bullet to his leg. Vince grabs the shotgun, blood pouring from his shoulder, he fires both barrels, taking Paco's head off.

Hearing the gunfire, Morelli and Muldoon run to the bar. Armand shoots Muldoon in the chest. Morelli shot the Hatian in the head. Willie aims his gun at the fallen Muldoon, but Pete shoots him under the arm with a 357-magnum blowing his heart out. Burt is looking to do something, but Nails busts him in the face with a hard right hand. Teeth fly out of his mouth. Burt, all fucked up, spits out blood and says,

"That's all ya got?" Nails smashes a bottle over Burt's head, then rams the jagged edges into his throat. Burt makes hideous noises as he chokes on his own blood.

Morelli is holding pressure on Muldoon's wound. "Call a fuckin ambulance", he yells.

Vince and Lenny are bleeding, Teddy is shaken.

Pete says "I can't believe I just saved that asshole's life. I gotta go, this piece isn't legal." Pete slipped out the backdoor.

The shootout was big news, five dead, three wounded. Teddy's Place was history. Teddy retired to Florida and got involved in direct to video porn VHS tapes. Vince recovered from his wounds but was devastated over Connie's murder. He and Teddy paid for her funeral. No charges were pressed on anyone. Vince kept working, but his heart wasn't in it. Eventually he partnered up with Teddy and his Video business.

Muldoon recovered and wisely, took early retirement. On 42nd Street, it was business as usual.

• • • •

Although this is all fiction, I based Teddy G on an ex-mobster, Teddy Gatsworth. According to my former boss at Liquidators, Teddy was a retired 'soldier'. He had his own line of porn VHS tapes that had the company by the name of TGA. (Teddy Gatsworth Associates). Norm used to trade with him and being that I ran his adult department. I dealt with Teddy a lot.

THE BLIZZARD

1

"You let that fat bastard in here again?" Big Willie was yelling at his barmaid, Gina.

"I'm working here alone during the day; I can't control who comes in and out of here nor can I follow them into the Men's room."

The fat bastard in question was Charlie Sabatini, aka Fat Sab. He was a weed dealer who graduated to dealing PCP. Problem was he was his own best customer.

Willie had kicked him out of the bar, but Sab wasn't having it. He just came in one night and stared Willie down. Willie was 6'10" and weighed 285 pounds. He was a former Golden Gloves Champion. Sab was 5' 8" and weighed close to 400 lbs. Willie said, "Didn't I tell you to stay out of here?"

A PCPed out Sab replied, "Think you're bad enough to keep me out?" That was it, Willie punched him in the face. No effect. Then he punted him in the balls. Patrons said it was field goal that lifted Sab off his feet and dropped him on his ass. Willie proceeded to kick the shit out of him.

That was about a week ago. Sab had a partner in his homemade PCP business, Greg. Greg was Stan Laurel to Sab's Oliver Hardy. Greg was a blonde guy, a beanpole at 145 pounds. His face was pockmarked from untreated acne. As most junkies do, the two had a falling out over money. Greg went to Sab's place with 5 gallons of gas and a hammer and nails. Then he went back where he got the gas and asked for a book of matches. The clerk stalled him off and called the cops. Greg was now in the Tombs on attempted arson charges.

"He's going to try and get even, Willie, he's crazy," Gina told him.

"I can't be here twenty-four seven," Willie told her. "Now I'm gonna have to hire a security guy when I'm not here."

"I'm sorry, Willie, the guy scares me," Gina confessed.

"It's on me," he admitted. "I should have booted him out the minute I knew he was dealing."

"He's been dealing since 1969, that was five years ago. It was just weed, then he started making his own poison", Gina finished. Gina was an Italian lady with short, dark hair, and a major league chest. She had two kids and no husband. She needed this job. "Did you hear the weather report", she asked Willie.

"No, what about it?"

"Going to be bad, a big Nor'easter. Storm of the century they say."

"It's always going to be the big one, then we get a dusting."

"I don't know, Boss, radio and news are all over this."

"I'd better go move my car in case they have to plow the lot."

Willie put on his coat and went out. Five minutes later, he was back and pissed.

"I got four fuckin flat tires, that motherfucker is dead." Willie took a three-foot piece of steel pipe and stormed out.

· · · ·

2

STEVE TERRY OWNED A garage and a snowplow. He was following the weather intently. He told his apprentice, Pete Christiano, to get the plow ready. Steve was a short, fat guy with a trimmed beard and glasses. Pete was a tall guy, over six feet, with shaggy red hair and a full beard. Pete was learning the mechanic's trade. Pete wasn't thrilled about working in the storm.

"Hope you ain't got any plans for tonight, Petey, if this storm is half as bad as they say it will be, we got a busy night."

"You don't know how thrilled I am to hear that", Pete muttered under his breath. "This guy wants an oil change and his tires rotated." Pete pointed to a '68 Eldorado. "Tell him to leave it and come back in a couple of hours."

Pete turned to the customer, who happened to be Charlie Sabatini.

"You heard him, give me your keys and come back later."

Charlie had his buddy, a guy called Gasoline, with him. Gasoline looked like S. Clay Wilson's Checkered demon with an Afro. Gasoline just had to say something. "C'mon, man, just do it now, we gots things to do."

Pete looked at him and said. "Well Pally, I gots things to do too, so fuck off and come back later."

Gasoline gave Pete a dirty look. "Gas", Sab said, "let's leave it, I have to grab something." The two left.

"When fuckers like that come in here, don't take your eyes off them," Steve told Pete.

"Yeah, I know, fuckin junkies," Pete muttered.

Just then Big Willie walked in. "Hey Steve O, I need road service. I got four flats and my car is in.... is that Charlie Sab's car?" Willie pointed to the Caddy.

"Yeah," said Steve. "He just, whoa what the fuck are you...."

Willie walked over to the Caddy and smashed the front window with the pipe. Then he took out the back window.

"Tell that fat cocksucker we're even. And come get my car." Willie stormed off.

"Great," muttered Steve. "Like we need to be in the middle of this pissing contest."

"Pete, put his fuckin car outside and leave the keys in it. We got plowing to do." It was now snowing heavily. Steve wrote a note and put it on the driver's seat. It said, "Willie said this was payback, sorry, not our fault."

"Last thing I need is that dust-head on my case," he muttered.

• • • •
3
AT MCGIRR'S POOL HALL, the cook, Pops, and the manager, Howard, wanted to close and get out before the storm got really bad.

Pops was a cranky older guy in his 70's, Howard was a bald guy, tall with black framed glasses. Only a few patrons remained. Nails Morgan and Cueball Jones were shooting a game of 8 ball. About a dozen empty longnecks were minding their table. Nails was a big tough guy who always looked a bit disheveled. Thick dark hair, a squashed nose, and sacred up forehead. He was known in the area as a man you didn't cross. Jones was the opposite. A tall, heavily muscled, black man with a shaved head and a flare for fashion. Jones was a pool hustler; Morgan was a strong-arm guy. They were an odd couple that got along.

"I should have never listened to you, that motherfucker, Darryl never comes though." Jones bluntly told Morgan.

"Sometimes he does."

"Name one time." Morgan thought a minute.

"I fuckin thought as much. Stay the fuck away from him, we just wasted the night and it's snowing like a bitch out there."

"Hot color TVs my ass, he's too fuckin stupid to get anything that good."

"Ok," Morgan gave ground, "I fucked up. Let's get out of here."

"Safe home, boys," Pops said and began turning out the lights hoping the last couple of patrons would take the hint.

The two got outside to find two feet of snow had already fallen. Jones looked up into the streetlight. The snow was blocking the light. "Sweet Baby Jesus for once the weatherman got it right," Jones exclaimed.

"How the hell are we going to get over to 14th Street? I don't see anything moving out here," Morgan bitched.

"Subway down the end of the block."

They trudged in knee high heavy snow; both were puffing like they ran a race when they got to the subway.

"I am really outta shape," Morgan gasped, "maybe we should join a gym?"

"No shit," huffed Jones. "What say we go to Gleason's Monday?"

"Yeah, if they don't find our frozen bodies in this shit."

"You ever the optimist?"

"My religion has nothing to do with a blizzard."

"You need to get yourself a dictionary."

"I'd probably use it to hit somebody. You know something, I don't think the trains are running."

Jones looked down the track. He didn't see any lights. "How long do you think we've been here?"

"Not long, maybe fifteen minutes or so." Jones looked at his watch. "Let's wait another fifteen."

"Then what? We'll freeze our balls off if we stay here."

"Not a lot of choices, and maybe no choices. The Harem, The Venus, Show World..."

"No offence, Jonsey, but staying overnight in a fuckin porn theater with a bunch of derelicts and perverts isn't high on my list right now. Besides, they are maybe five fucking blocks away."

"Alright, one chance is that Willie's may be open. That's two blocks over, one block down, are you up for it?"

"The thought of alcoholic beverages is a great motivation for me."

"Let's go then."

The storm had gotten worse. Pellets of ice mixed with the snow and hit their faces like needles. They made one block, then Jones slipped and went down hard. Nails rushed to help him up. Jones couldn't stand.

"I broke my damn leg." He groaned. "I can't put any weight on it." Nails picked him up in a fireman's carry.

"What the hell are you doing?"

I'm doing what my people have been doing for years, carrying the black man."

"You know your honky ass is dead when you put me down, right?"

"Promises, promises, let's just hope he's open."

• • • •

4

ON 8TH AVENUE, SHOW World was still open as patrons and staff were stranded there. Most has left when the snow got heavy. The rest were stuck there, or they could cross the street and try Port Authority, but nothing was running, even the cabs. The night manager was Robert Denardo, a no-nonsense guy who felt he should be in a better position. At 5'9" with slicked back black hair, and a roman nose, he didn't relish the idea of being stuck there.

Lucinda was a 25-year-old Puerto Rican girl who worked the Dial A Doll booths. Lucinda or 'Luce' as she called herself, was top heavy with a bubble butt and a hard, Asian looking face. The trick was to get guys in the booth where a large pane of plexiglass separated her from the customer. It was a dollar for a minute. Luce would strip, play with herself, and keep the customer feeding dollars into the slot while they jerked off. Luce would get sleazy, using dildos, beer bottles, even a hairbrush to liven things up.

Her 'partner' was Dawn, a striking 6' black lady with a tight, toned body. Dawn had a medium Afro, and a few tats, one close to her pussy. She was a hit with submissive white men as she was a dominatrix as well as a booth girl. Her presence with these guys was so overpowering that she kept them feeding dollars into the slots. Dawn and Lucida were into each other as they had a complete disdain for men.

Their disdain was taken out on the creepy mop and pail guy, Mikey. Mikey was barely five feet tall. He had a face like the guy on the Lucky Charms box, unruly brown hair and a wispy mustache. Mikey's job was to mop up the cum in the peep booths. Mikey was fascinated by Luce, who would fuck with him. After her set, he would be doing something that required him to stoop down. Luce would make sure that her pussy was in his face. "You disgust me," he'd tell her. She would stick her finger in her twat, then put it in his mouth.

He'd spit and curse her out. Problem with Mikey is that he was conflicted. He was a self-loathing closeted man, who couldn't find his way out of the closet. After working at Show World for the last few months, he hated it. He would have to check each booth every time someone exited and mop up anything left behind. Some of the patrons called him 'load boy', which made him very angry.

Luce was talking about how they were stuck here. "Dis fucking weatherman got dis one right," she muttered.

"Yeah, and we won't be makin' any cash tonight, sweetheart," Dawn said.

Seeing that Mikey was watching, Luce went behind Dawn and wrapped her arms around her, slipping a hand into her bikini bottom. Mikey turned red and tried to look away. Luce's fingers slid into dawn's honey pot; Dawn gave a little moan of pleasure. Luce whispered in her ear, "Let's give the boys a little show." Dawn nodded and they walked to a revolving stage with a mattress on it. Luce looked at Mickey, who was almost drooling.

• • • •

5

STEVE AND PETE GOT to the first lot. "No cars left here that's good," Steve commented.

"I really think we shoulda let this play out and start when it stopped," Pete muttered.

"Hey, smart guy, I can charge them for plowing it twice if I start now, get it? I'll make double."

"Yeah, sure whatever."

"Get that spotlight and get in the back, I need to see what I'm doing here."

"Me get in the bed with the spotlight. Oh, yeah, this just gets better and fuckin better."

"Just do it and stop bitching, the headlights keep getting covered up." Pete knew arguing was futile. He grabbed the big, battery powered spotlight and climbed into the bed of the truck.

"Hold it steady while I make the first pass," Steve ordered.

"Aye, aye, skipper," Pete muttered. He balanced the light on the roof of the cab. Steve made one pass, then backed up for another. He hit the gas and plowed through about three feet of packed snow. Then the plow lurched to a stop. Pete went flying over the cab and into a pile of snow.

"He's fuckin dead," Steve yelped and bailed out to see if Pete was alive.

Pete staggered to his feet. "What the hell happened," Pete asked. He was dazed and limping.

"I hit something under the snow"

"No shit? I would have never guessed."

"Are you alright?"

"I'm not sure, I don't think I broke anything but I'm too fuckin cold to really feel anything." Pete spit out blood.

"Get in the truck, I'll take you to Saint Vincent's."

They got in the truck, but they couldn't back it up. Wheels spun and pieces of tire flew off.

"Steve, back off, let's see what it is." Pete took the spotlight and went to look. Steve hit the edge of a steel plate, it punched though the plow blade.

"This is really fucked up, Bro, the truck is stuck, that plate weighs a ton, we need a sledgehammer or a torch to free it."

"Neither of which we have." Steve looked at the street sign.

"We aren't far from Willie's place, let hope he's open, ain't like we can do anything tonight."

The two started walking to Willie's.

Around this time Fat Sab and Gasoline went to get Sab's car. Sab went ballistic when he saw it.

"My fuckin Caddy, what did those cocksuckers do to my car?" Sab surveyed the damage, then saw the note.

"Willie did this, that fat motherfucker did this, I'm going to kill his ass now."

"Sab, calm the fuck down," Gasoline said. Both were whacked out on

dust and Sab was losing it.

"You calm down you worthless piece of shit, it ain't your car that's trashed."

Sab popped open the trunk and started tossing stuff out until he found what he had stashed, a sawed-off double-barreled shotgun.

"Are you fuckin crazy," Gas asked.

"They fucked up my car. You going with me? You'd better be going with me."

Gas was now scared for his life. "Yeah, Buddy, I'll be right behind you."

They started walking in the blizzard. Gas walked slow until he could barely see Sab. Then he ducked down into the subway platform. "I'd rather freeze then get caught up in his shit," he said to himself.

· · · ·

6

WILLIE WANTED TO CLOSE, but no one had picked up his car. "Helluva a thing," he said to Gina. "Looks like we're stuck here."

"Nothing we can do; this is one nasty storm," she replied.

Just then the door opened, and a big, snow-covered figure came into the bar. Actually, two snow covered figures. Morgan dumped Jones on a bar stool.

"Gina, give us a couple of shots." Gina hurried to comply.

"Hope you guys didn't get frost bite," she said, a bit concerned.

"No, no frost bite, but do you have a gun here? I need to shoot this racist honky faggot." Jones said shaking from the cold. Nails threw back his shot and looked hard at Jones.

"Ya know something, if I knew it would come to this, I would have picked my own cotton." The two stared hard at each other, then burst out laughing.

"That's a good one Nails, did you just make it up?"

"Yeah, actually I did, let's look at your leg."

It was Jones's right leg. Gina pulled his boot off. His ankle was grotesquely swollen.

"It's a bad sprain," she told him. "Let's pack it in ice."

"You sure about that?"

"I got two boys, seen enough sprains over the years. You'll be ok, just need to get the swelling down, then wrap it up. Your ladies will need a new dance partner for a couple of weeks."

"When this storm stops, Nails can take me over to my lady Wanda's crib, she'll nurse me back to health," Jones explained.

Nails thought about Wanda and her 42D chest. "Yeah, she'll be nursing you a lot."

"Get me another shot." The door flew open, and two more snow men staggered in, Steve and Pete.

"Thank God you're open," Steve gasped. Gina put a shot in front of each of them.

"Did you get my car," Willie asked.

"No", Pete cut in, "and you really don't want to hear that story, but let's just say that nothing is getting done until this fuckin storm lets up, right Steve?"

"Willie, I jumped the gun and fucked up. Now my truck is stuck too." "Great, just wonderful, what else could go wrong?"

A lot was about to go wrong. Fat Sab kicked open the door.

"You're a fuckin' dead man", he screamed, then pointed the sawed off at Willie. He let loose one barrel. Willie, moving fast for a guy his size, ducked into the cooler. A couple of pellets hit his shoulder. Sab was half frozen but went for another shot. Pete winged a full bottle of something at him and hit him in the head. Sab shook it off. "I never liked you, Pete." Sab aimed at Pete, but Nails was up and attempted to tackle him.

Nails hit him at his waist and slammed Sab into the wall.

Sab clubbed Nails on the back with the shotgun. Nails backed up, then busted Sab in the side of the head with a hard right fist. Steve yanked the gun out of Sab's hand. Sab was now dazed. Willie opened the door to the cooler;

it took all four men to shove him in and lock the door. "Anything valuable in there," Steve asked.

"Nothing but two kegs, didn't get my delivery obviously," Willie told him.

Sab was howling and smashing something against the door. Nails picked up the shotgun. "I'd shoot him, but that might just piss him off, more."

"Listen to that motherfucker," said Jones, "maybe he's a werewolf."

"He's all fucked up on his own shit, that's what he is." Willie summed it up. "We don't let him out, minute this storm slows down, I call the cops, I'm not fuckin around with this asshole anymore."

"How bad is your shoulder, Boss," Gina asked.

"He nicked me, it had to be birdshot."

"Let me see it." Willie peeled off his sweatshirt. He had two little holes in his shoulder. Gina took a closer look, then got her purse. "I need tweezers."

Gina took some Vodka, cleaned off the blood, then used the tweezers to pull two pellets out. "Bird shot, you are lucky."

"Luckier than that asshole, I'm pressing charges, I'll get him and his fuckin dope off the street."

Willie thought about it for a moment.

"Ya know what, I'm calling the cops now."

• • • •

7

LUCE AND DAWN STARTED making out. A couple of patrons and employees watched. Luce and Dawn started swapping spit. Dawn pulled Luce's top off and sucked an erect nipple. Luce shoved her hand down into Dawn's panties and fish hooked her pussy. Dawn gasped and shoved her tongue down Luce's throat. Mikey had sweat dripping off his face. The two hit the mattress and wrestled around on it.

A few people had grabbed folding chairs and were sitting around the mattress. Dawn had Luce on her back and was pulling her panties off. Luce struggled so Dawn sat on her face and rubbed her pussy in it.

Heavy breathing filled the air. Denardo had a frown on his face, this was money not being earned. He was going to stop it, then he thought better of it. He would talk to them about doing this in the Triple Threat Theater upstairs.

Now the two were eating each other out. "Lick her asshole," someone yelled. Luce ran her tongue over Dawn's rosebud. It was slick from her juices. One of the other booth girls tossed them a double headed dildo. Their faces slick with each other's juices, they scrambled for the sex toy. Mikey inched closer, rubbing his crotch. The women played with the dildo. Dawn used it to fuck Luce. Luce moaned loudly as it was thrust deep inside her.

"I want to fuck your ass with this thing," Luce blurted out. Dawn bent over as Luce lubed up her ass with her tongue. Luce slid the dildo into her ass. "Too deep," yelled Dawn. But Luce held it in, tickling Dawn's throbbing clit with her finger.

"I'm gonna cum, you fuckin whore, I'm going to cum!" Dawn's back arched as she screamed and came. She fell back on the mattress, her pussy still throbbing.

Luce sat on a chair, getting herself off with her hand. Mikey was also still rubbing himself. "C'mere you little bitch," Luce taunted him. Mikey didn't move. "I told you to get over here, look at my pussy." Mikey got closer, then real close. Luce's finger worked furiously, sweat poured down her face, and then she came, right in Mikey's face. Luce was a squirter. Mikey screamed like acid was tossed in his face. Mikey tried to wipe his face. Luce was laughing hysterically. So was everyone else. Denardo chuckled "Might be a new career for ya, Mikey boy."

"Fuck you," Mikey screamed, "Fuck all of yous."

"Calm down kid, she was just joking with you."

"The fuck she was, fuck you fuck her and fuck this place."

Mikey ran over to Luce and spit in her face.

"Why you little cocksucker, I'll kill you," Luce screamed.

Mikey ran to the front door, but it was locked. Luce was right behind him. He ran through the small bookshop, and out onto 42nd Street. The snow was so heavy that it was close to a white out. Mikey turned and gave Luce the finger. He never saw the snowplow that ran him over.

• • • •

8

THE STORM BROKE ABOUT 3AM. Willie had called the police and told them that he had Charlie Sabatini locked in his cooler. He told them that Charlie tried to kill him, and he had witnesses. Steve and Pete had to go retrieve their plow. Nails and Jones hung out waiting for the cops.

"Thanks for hangin' around guys," Willie told them.

"You gave us weary travelers shelter, it's the least myself and my man Friday can do," Nail's told him.

"You're still on this shit," Jones muttered

"Well, you can't chase me, so that sorta gives me incentive to break your balls."

"Fuck you and the horse you rode in on. Say, the beast has been quiet maybe he's dead."

"Think you froze him, Willie?"

"I wish, but that's just a big fridge."

Nails looked outside. "Law just pulled up."

Three officers walked inside. "I'm Sgt. Jenkins, you have Mr. Sabatini on ice for me?"

"Yes officer, we do, but he was PCPed out last night so maybe you best be ready when we open the cooler." Jenkins took out a can of Mace.

"Not for nothing," Nails chimed in, "that ain't even gonna slow him down."

"Well, we can't just shoot him,"

"Why the hell not, he tried to shoot us." Nails pointed to the shotgun. "We didn't touch it; his prints are on it."

"Bag that," Jenkins told one of the patrolmen. Jenkins took out a Billy club.

"Open it," he ordered.

Willie opened it and stepped back. A horrible figure stood there naked.

Sab was bloody and his hands were busted. He beat the two kegs until they busted, beer smell filled the air. Nails glared at him. "So, this is the great shit that you're pushing? Well look what it did to you."

Sab rolled his eye and glared at everyone. "You people don't know how much trouble you're in," he muttered.

Jenkins called an ambulance and Sab was taken for evaluation. He was going away for quite some time.

"What a morning," Jenkins said to no one. "First a mop boy from Show world gets turned into road pizza, now this."

• • • •

This blizzard happened; it might have been 1978. I was the Pete who got thrown off the truck. I was a mechanic back then and we were out plowing. It was too much. We did spend the night at a bar called The Poor House in Lyndhurst, New Jersey.

Sab was real. He was a pot dealer, and I was a customer. He got involved in the PCP crap and his partner did try to burn his house down. He did get into a brawl with a bar owner named Willie. He pulled a bag of product out when an off-duty cop spotted him. It took six cops to take him down. He did five years. He died at age 49.

SLAMBURGER

The building was a steal, we bought it at a rock bottom price. It was where Show World was located. Show World was a porn superstore with three floors. It was brightly lit and garish. There were film peep shows, live peep shows, Video peeps, Dial A Doll booths, and the Ultra Burlesque theater which featured name porn stars and strippers. Downstairs was TV City featuring Pre-Op transsexuals in booths.

In short, Show World catered to every perversion. Though not as extreme or as skuzzy as Peepland or Peep O Rama, Show World had its moments. Like a guy walking in and emptying a revolver into a 'buddy booth' because his boyfriend was blowing another guy. Or an older guy having a heart attack while rubbing one out in a booth. Then there was one of the booth girls keeling over from a massive overdose as she flashed potential customers.

By the late 80's, early 90's, everything had gotten dangerous. Crack cocaine fueled it. Girls would leave their stations to score some rock and never finish their shifts. Decay set in as the owner knew the place's days were numbered. The staff, lost interest in keeping the place up.

When the owner died in 2018, the building was closed and put up for sale. With everything catering to tourists, why not sell hamburgers?

The place was gutted. Years of crusted semen was scraped off the floors. Booths were busted up and hauled away. Whatever was left of DVDs, players, equipment, video monitors, office furniture etc., was put up for auction. The rest filled huge dumpsters. A guy named Ralph would be the manager. Ralph thought this would be his big break. He hired cooks, cashiers, and a wait staff. He knew that being on the corner of 42nd Street and 8th avenue was a great location. What no one figured on was the ghosts.

It started before the place opened. Christy, one of the cashiers, heard a low moaning sound coming from the Women's Rest Room.

She opened the door and saw a woman sitting on the toilet playing with herself. The women looked at Christy with dead eyes and moaned "Lick my pussy you little bitch." Christy was out the door and into Ralph's office. "You have to get this psycho out of here," she said.

"What psycho," asked Ralph.

"The one in the rest room playing with herself, she must have snuck in."

"I don't see how she got in, but let's take a look."

They went to the stall and Christy opened the door. "God, it smells like the East River at high tide," gasped Ralph. Christy looked like she was going to hurl.

"Get Jose in here with a mop and some Fabreez," he ordered. "Not a word about this, ok?"

"Seriously, Ralph, what the fuck?"

"What the fuck is right, I'm thinking she is hiding somewhere in here. Let's search the place." They found no one. They went back to Ralph's office.

"I don't know where she went, but she's not here," Christy said. "And I didn't imagine it, the crazy bitch asked me to lick her."

"Clear your head, what did she look like?"

"She was blonde, with big hair and she was wearing high, white boots and some purple lingerie."

"You just described a 70's Go-Go dancer".

"Well that's what she was wearing, this is fucked up."

"Ok, I am at a loss here. Obviously, someone snuck in. Just make sure the doors are locked at all times."

"I'll tell the crew."

"Thanks, I have to go over these applications."

Christy left. Ralph needed to hire a couple of bus boys. He scanned the applications and noticed he was not alone. A very effeminate looking man was in front of his desk. Ralph thought he was applying for a job.

"Can I help you?"
"Where is Freddy?" "Who is Freddy?"
"My boyfriend, that douche shot us."
"Excuse me?"
"Freddy was giving me some inspired head when Dougie came in and shot us."
"You were shot, then how..." Ralph noticed the man had bullet holes in
his face.
"Jesus Christ who the fuck are you?"
"I'm Wayne, is Freddy blowing you too?"
"What the fuck, Jose, get in here and take this fucker to the street, Ralph bellowed.
Jose ran into the office to find Ralph and no one else.
"Trouble, Boss?"
"Did you just see a guy leave here?"
"No, I just heard you yell for me and here I am."
"Do you know anyone left from the old days, you know, when this place was Show World?"
"There was this lady, a fortune teller, a Strega."
"What's a Strega?"
"A witch, it's an Italian witch. She had a place in a loft, now she is in the West Village. Her name is Julia."
"Can you find her?"
"Yeah, but why?"
Ralph told Jose about what happened with Christy.
"That's some fucked up shit."
"Tell me about it, now go get her."
Jose returned with an old woman dressed in black. She had to be about 80. Jose introduced her. "Ralph, this is Julia." Ralph went to shake her hand, but Julia glared at him.
"Fucked up big time, didn't ya?"

"What do you mean?"

"A guy wrote an article about this street years ago, he called it The Devil's Playground. And it was, evil lived here, and you can't get rid of evil. It's like shining shit, cover it up, it still stinks. Everything on the block stunk. From the movie theaters to places like this," she cackled. "I worked here, hell I worked all around here for over 50 years. I know all the secrets."

Ralph stuttered "I think we have a ghost."

"I know you do, and more than one." Julia got on the floor and put her ear to it.

"I can hear the ghosts of a billion sperm cells crying out. I feel the people who died here, and they aren't happy to have their home ripped up."

"Can you help get rid of them?"

"No, I won't even try. Your corporations ruined it all, you destroyed our way of life and made it a tourist sucker trap. Disney," she spat that word out. "They were the real plague, and Rudolph Giuliani, they were the ones who orchestrated this travesty. Now the butcher bill is due, have fun paying it." She stormed off.

"She's a fuckin nut," Ralph said. Jose just crossed himself.

"We open tomorrow, I'm not going to believe this shit anymore, someone is playing games."

Jose just shook his head. "Whatever you say Boss."

For the Grand Opening, America's Mayor, Rudolph Giuliani would be present. It seemed fitting as he was the guy who orchestrated the gentrification of 42nd Street. Giuliani had a table in the back so he could press flesh and forward his agenda. The place was packed with line of people waiting to get in. Ralph was ecstatic, the turnout was great. Everything ran smooth for the first couple of hours. Then a 'waiter' appeared at the former Mayor's table.

"Would The Mayor like to try my special sauce," he asked.

"Sure," he said, "I'll give it a taste."

The waiter pulled his cock out and jerked off on Rudy's burger.

"For Christ's sake, are you insane," Rudy bellowed.

The waiter vanished, but was replaced by a guy with bullet holes in his face.

"Did Freddy blow you too," he asked.

Rudy got to his feet, ready to fight the guy when a woman ran screaming out of the rest room. She was followed by a masturbating booth girl moaning, "lick my pussy, you prissy bitch." Ralph went to grab her and went right though her. The waiter kept appearing at people's tables jerking off into their burgers.

People were screaming and there was a loud rumbling. The floor cracked open, and a horde of ghostly masturbators came though led by the former dead publisher of Screw Magazine, Al Goldstein. "We're coming to get you, Rudy, I put the Goldstein curse on you," Al moaned.

The ghostly horde surrounded Rudy while pulling their puds. Patrons and staff ran out the front door. Ralph stood helplessly as a river of semen poured out the front door. "Make it stop, he moaned, please make it stop."

"Ralph, wake up, you're having a nightmare." Ralph was in bed with his wife in their apartment.

"Jesus," Ralph muttered, shaking, "That was a weird fuckin dream."

"Better get going, dear," his wife said, "Today is your big day."

"Yeah," said Ralph, "Grand opening and all that." Ralph showered and dressed, then took the subway to 8th Avenue. Trashburger was all decked out and ready to go. Ralph entered with a big smile on his face.

That smile vanished when Christy marched up to him and said, "We just had a problem in the Ladies Rest Room."

• • • •

Obviously, this was all tongue in cheek. When I learned that Smash Burger now occupied the former location of Show World, we all had a big laugh. Then Nick my editor suggested this be a story, and I went with it. Al Goldstein and Rudy Giuliani hated each other. Goldstien had Rudy on the cover of Screw close to a dozen times. When both Al and I were at the Sexpo at The Javittes Center, Giuliani was livid as this snuck in right under his nose. We watched him outside ranting to the press about this sleazy event. Al turned to me and said, "This is a classy event, the only thing sleazy here is me...and you." The 'Goldstein Curse' was what Al used on his enemies, and it worked, he beat Pan Am Airlines and Pillsbury in court. Plus, several former mayors and prosecutors. RIP Al, we miss you.

About the Author

Pete Chiarella has written for Screw Magazine, Chiller Theater Magazine, Shock Cinema, Something Weird Video Blue Book Vol. 1 & 2, Ultraviolent Magazine, Uncut, Dangerous Encounters, Spaghetti Western Digest and Sleaze Fiend Magazine. He also helmed twenty issues of his own magazine, Grindhouse Purgatory. He has a new magazine out now called Grindhouse Resurrection!

OTHER WORKS INCLUDE
42nd Street Pete's Big Book of Grindhouse Trivia
Gunfighters of the Drunken Master trilogy
A Whole Bag of Crazy

Ingram Content Group UK Ltd.
Milton Keynes UK
UKHW010638120623
423291UK00001B/83